Agatha Raisin
and
Love, Lies and Liquor

D1151477

The Agatha Raisin series
(listed in order)

Agatha Raisin
and
Love, Lies and Liquor

M. C. Beaton

ROBINSON
London

Constable & Robinson Ltd
3 The Lanchesters
162 Fulham Palace Road
London W6 9ER
www.constablerobinson.com

First published in the USA in 2006 by St Martin's Press
175 Fifth Avenue, New York, NY 10010

First UK edition published by Constable,
an imprint of Constable & Robinson Ltd 2006

This paperback edition published by Robinson,
an imprint of Constable & Robinson Ltd 2007

A copy of the British Library Cataloguing in
Publication data is available from the British Library

ISBN: 978-1-84529-448-9 (pbk)
ISBN: 978-1-84529-444-1 (hbk)

Printed and bound in the EU

1 3 5 7 9 10 8 6 4 2

This book is dedicated to
Sue and Rod Close,
with affection.

Chapter One

James Lacey, Agatha Raisin's ex-husband with whom she was still in love, had come back into her life. He had moved into his old cottage next door to Agatha's.

But although he seemed interested in Agatha's work at her detective agency, not a glint of love lightened his blue eyes. Agatha dressed more carefully than she had done in ages and spent a fortune at the beautician's, but to no avail. This was the way, she thought sadly, that things had been before. She felt as if some cruel hand had wound the clock of time backwards.

Just when Agatha was about to give up, James called on her and said friends of his had moved into Ancombe and had invited them both to dinner. His host, he said, was a Mr David Hewitt who was retired from the Ministry of Defence. His wife was called Jill.

Delighted to be invited as a couple, Agatha set out with James from their thatched cottages in the village of Carsely in the Cotswolds to drive the short distance to Ancombe.

The lilac blossom was out in its full glory.

Wisteria and clematis trailed down the walls of honey-coloured cottages, and hawthorn, the fairy tree, sent out a heady sweet smell in the evening air.

Agatha experienced a qualm of nervousness as she drove them towards Ancombe. She had made a few visits to James in his cottage, but they were always brief. James was always occupied with something and seemed relieved when she left. Agatha planned to make the most of this outing. She was dressed in a biscuit-coloured suit with a lemon-coloured blouse and high-heeled sandals. Her brown hair gleamed and shone.

James was wearing a tweed sports jacket and flannels. 'Am I overdressed?' asked Agatha.

One blue eye swivelled in her direction. 'No, you look fine.'

The Hewitts lived in a bungalow called Merrydown. As Agatha drove up the short gravelled drive, she could smell something cooking on charcoal. 'It's not a barbecue?' she asked.

'I believe it is. Here we are.'

'James, if you had told me it was a barbecue, I would have dressed more suitably.'

'Don't nag,' said James mildly, getting out of the car.

Agatha detested barbecues. Barbecues were for Americans, Australians and Polynesians, or any of those other people with a good climate. The English, from her experience, delighted in undercooked meat served off paper plates in an insect-ridden garden.

James rang the doorbell. The door was opened by a small woman with pinched little features and pale grey eyes. Her grey hair was dressed in girlish curls. She was wearing a print frock and low-heeled sandals.

'James, darling!' She stretched up and enfolded him in an embrace. 'And who is this?'

'Don't you remember, I was told to bring my ex-wife along. This is Agatha Raisin. Agatha, Jill.'

Jill linked her arm in James's, ignoring Agatha. 'Come along. We're all in the garden.' Agatha trailed after them. She wanted to go home.

Various people were standing around the garden drinking some sort of fruit cup. Agatha, who felt in need of a strong gin and tonic, wanted more than ever to flee.

She was introduced to her host, who was cooking dead things on the barbecue. He was wearing a joke apron with a picture of a woman's body in a corset and fishnet stockings. James was taken round and introduced to the other guests, while Agatha stood on a flagged patio teetering on her high heels.

Agatha sighed and sank down into a garden chair. She opened her handbag and took out her cigarettes and lighter and lit a cigarette.

'Do you mind awfully?' Her host stood in front of her, brandishing a knife.

'What?'

'This is a smoke-free zone.'

Agatha leaned round him and stared at the barbecue. Black smoke was beginning to pour out from something on the top. 'Then you'd better get a fire extinguisher,' said Agatha. 'Your food is burning.'

He let out a squawk of alarm and rushed back to the barbecue. Agatha blew a perfect smoke ring. She felt her nervousness evaporating. She did not care what James thought. Jill was a dreadful hostess, and worse than that, she seemed to have a thing about James. So Agatha sat placidly, smoking and dreaming of the moment when the evening would be over.

There was one sign of relief. A table was carried out into the garden and chairs set about it. She had dreaded having to stand on the grass in her spindly heels, eating off a paper plate.

Jill had reluctantly let go of James's arm and gone into the house. She reappeared with two of the women guests carrying wine bottles and glasses. 'Everyone to the table,' shouted David.

Agatha crushed out her cigarette on the patio stones and put the stub in her handbag. By the time she had heaved herself out of her chair, it was to find that James was seated next to Jill and another woman, and she was left to sit next to a florid-faced man who gave her a goggling stare and then turned to chat to the woman on his other side.

David put a plate of blackened charred things in front of Agatha. She helped herself to a glass of wine. The conversation became general, everyone talking about people Agatha did not know. Then she caught the name Andrew Lloyd Webber. 'I do like his musicals,' she said, glad to be able to talk about something.

There was a little startled silence and then Jill said in a patronizing voice, 'But his music is so derivative.'

'All music is derivative,' said Agatha.

'Dear me,' tittered one of the female guests. 'You'll be saying you like Barry Manilow next.'

'Why not?' asked Agatha truculently. 'He's a great performer. Got some good tunes, too.' There was a startled silence and then everyone began to talk at once.

I will never understand the Gloucestershire middle classes, thought Agatha. Oh, well, might as well eat. She sliced a piece of what appeared to be chicken. Blood oozed out on to her plate.

James was laughing at something Jill was saying. He had not once looked in her direction. He had abandoned her as soon as they entered the house.

Suddenly a thought hit Agatha, a flash of the blindingly obvious. I do not need to stay here. These people are rude and James is a disgrace. She rose and went into the house. 'Second door on your left,' Jill shouted after her, assuming Agatha wanted to go to the toilet.

Agatha went straight through the house and outside. She got into her car and drove off. Let James find his own way home.

When she reached her cottage, she let herself in, went through to the kitchen and kicked off her sandals. Her cats circled her legs in welcome. 'I've had a God-awful time,' she told them.

'James has finally been and gone and done it. I've grown up at last. I don't care if I never see him again.'

'What an odd woman!' Jill was exclaiming. 'To go off like that without a word.'

'Well, you did rather cut her dead,' said James uneasily. 'I mean, she was left on her own, not knowing anyone.'

'But one doesn't introduce people at parties any more.'

'You introduced me.'

'Oh, James, sweetie. Don't go on. Such weird behaviour.' But the evening for James was ruined. He now saw these people through Agatha Raisin's small bearlike eyes.

'I'd better go and see if she's all right,' he said, getting to his feet.

'I'll drive you,' said Jill.

'No, please don't. It would be rude of you to leave your guests. I'll phone for a taxi.'

James rang Agatha's doorbell, but she did not answer. He tried phoning but got no reply. He left a message for her to call back, but she did not.

He shrugged. Agatha would come around. She always did.

But to his amazement the days grew into weeks and Agatha continued to be chilly towards him. She turned down invitations to dinner, saying

12

she was 'too busy'. He had met Patrick Mulligan one day in the village stores. Patrick worked for Agatha and he told James they were going through a quiet period.

When Sir Charles Fraith came to stay with Agatha, James began to be really worried. Charles, he knew, had once had an affair with Agatha. He dropped in and out of her life, occasionally helping her with cases. For the first time, James realized with amazement, he felt jealous. He had always taken it for granted that Agatha would remain, as far as he was concerned, her usual doting self. Something would have to be done.

'So how's your ex?' asked Charles one Saturday as he and Agatha sat in her garden.

'I told you. I neither know nor care. I told you about that terrible barbecue.'

'They sound like shiters but we all know weird people.'

'He abandoned me! And when they all started sniggering about Andrew Lloyd Webber, he did nothing to defend me.'

'Oh, well. It's nice to see you off the hook. If you are off the hook.'

But Agatha was addicted to obsessions. Without one going on in her head, she was left with herself, a state of affairs she did not enjoy.

'So no murders these days?' asked Charles.

'Not a one. Nothing but lost teenagers and cats and dogs. I feel guilty. I persuaded young Harry Beam, Mrs Freedman's nephew, to stay with me another year before going to university. He's finding things very dull.'

'Is everyone else still with you?'

'Yes, Mrs Freedman is still secretary. Then there's Harry, Phil Marshall and Patrick Mulligan as detectives.'

'Why don't you take some time off? Go away somewhere. Get away from brooding about him next door.'

'*I am not brooding about him next door!*'

Charles was so self-contained and neat in his impeccably tailored clothes and well-cut fair hair that Agatha sometimes felt like striking him. Nothing seemed to ruffle Charles's calm surface. She often wondered what he really thought of her.

'Anyway,' Agatha went on, 'I'm taking time off from the office today. Mrs Freedman will phone me if anything dramatic happens. What's wrong with Andrew Lloyd Webber anyway?'

'Don't ask me. I never could understand the middle classes.'

Fuelled by jealousy, James did not pause to think whether he really wanted the often-infuriating Agatha back in his life. He watched and waited until Charles left and then watched some more

14

until he saw Agatha leaving her cottage on foot. He shot out of his own door to waylay her.

'Hello, James,' said Agatha, her small eyes like two pebbles. 'I'm just going down to the village stores.'

'I'll walk with you. I have a proposition to make.'

'This is so sudden,' said Agatha cynically.

'Stop walking so quickly. I feel we got off to a bad start. It really was quite a dreadful barbecue. So I have a suggestion to make. If you're not too busy at the office, we could take a holiday together.'

Agatha's heart began to thump and she stopped dead under the shade of a lilac tree.

'I thought I would surprise you and take you off somewhere special that was once very dear to me. You see, I may have told you I've given up writing military history. I now write travel books.'

'Where did you think of?' asked Agatha, visions of Pacific islands and Italian villages racing through her brain.

'Ah, it is going to be a surprise.'

Agatha hesitated. But then she knew if she refused, she would never forgive herself. 'All right. What clothes should I take?'

'Whatever you usually take on holiday.'

'And when would we leave?'

'As soon as possible. Say, the end of next week?'

'Fine. Where are you going?'

'Back home to make some phone calls.'

Inside her cottage, Agatha looked at the phone and then decided she simply must communicate such marvellous news to her friend Mrs Bloxby, the vicar's wife. She let her cats out into the garden and then hurried off to the vicarage.

With her grey hair and gentle face, Mrs Bloxby always acted like a sort of balm on the turmoil of Agatha's feelings.

'Come in, Mrs Raisin,' she said. 'You are all flushed.'

Both Agatha and Mrs Bloxby were members of the Carsely Ladies' Society and it was an old-fashioned tradition among the members that only second names should be used.

'We'll sit in the garden,' said Mrs Bloxby, leading the way. 'Such a glorious day. Coffee?'

'No, don't bother.' Agatha sat down in a garden chair and Mrs Bloxby took the seat opposite her. Please let it not be anything to do with James, prayed Mrs Bloxby. I do so hope she's got over that.

'It's James!' exclaimed Agatha, and Mrs Bloxby's heart sank.

'I thought you were never going to have anything to do with him again.'

'Oh, it was because of that terrible party that I told you about. Well, just listen to this. He is arranging to take me on holiday.'

'Where?'

16

'It's to be a surprise.'

'Is that such a good idea? It might be some-where you'll hate.'

'He's a travel writer now and travel writers don't write about dreary places. I must lose weight if I'm going to look good on the beach.'

'But how do you know you are going to the beach?'

Agatha began to feel cross. 'Look, he obviously wants to make it a romantic holiday. You're a bit depressing about all this.'

Mrs Bloxby sighed. 'Of course I hope you will have a wonderful time. It's just . . .'

'What?' snapped Agatha.

'It's just that James has always behaved like a confirmed bachelor and he can be quite self-centred. This holiday will be what he wants, not what he would think you would like.'

Agatha rose angrily to her feet. 'Well, sage of the ages, I'm off to do some shopping.'

'Don't be angry with me,' pleaded Mrs Bloxby. 'I most desperately don't want to see you getting hurt again.' But the slamming of the garden door was her only reply.

Agatha threw herself into a fever of shopping: new swimsuit, filmy evening dress, beach clothes and beach bag. In her fantasies, James and she stood on the terrace of a hotel, looking out at the moonlight on the Mediterranean. He took her in his arms, his voice husky with desire and he said, 'I've always loved you.'

17

Patrick Mulligan, Phil Marshall and Harry Beam all assured her they could easily cope in her absence.

When the great day of departure arrived, she could hear James tooting angrily on the car horn as she packed and repacked. At last, heaving a suitcase that was so heavy it felt as if it had an anvil in it, she emerged from her cottage. The lover of her fantasies fled, to be replaced by the very real and present James Lacey. He lifted her suitcase into the boot and said, 'I thought you were going to be in there all day.'

'Well, here I am,' said Agatha brightly.

Agatha had been unable to sleep the previous night because of excitement. Shortly after they had driven off, she fell into a heavy sleep. After two hours, she awoke with a start. Rain was smearing the windscreen. The scenery seemed to consist of factories.

'Are we at the airport yet?' she asked.

'We're not going to the airport. Shut up, Agatha. This is supposed to be a surprise.'

Must be going to take the ferry, thought Agatha. Oh, how marvellous it would be to get out of dreary grey England and into the foreign sunshine. The factories and then some villas gave way to rain-swept countryside where wet sheep huddled in the shelter of drystone walls. A kestrel sailed overhead like a harbinger of doom.

'Where are we?' asked Agatha.

'Sussex.'

'Which Channel ferry runs from Sussex?'

'Don't spoil the surprise, Agatha, by asking questions.'

With rising apprehension, Agatha watched the miles of rain-soaked countryside go by. Were they going to Brighton? Now that would be really unoriginal.

James drove along a cliff road, then turned off. After two miles, he pulled into the side of the road in front of a sign that said 'Snoth-on-Sea'.

'This is the surprise,' he said portentously. 'This is one of the last unspoilt seaside resorts in Britain. I used to come here as a boy with my parents. Beautiful place. You'll love it.'

Agatha was stricken into silence, thinking of all the light clothes and beachwear and all the bottles of suntan lotion, face creams and make-up that were weighing down her suitcase. She tried to get Mrs Bloxby's gentle voice out of her head. 'This holiday will be what he wants, not what he would think you would like.'

James drove slowly down into the town, prepared to savour every moment. On the outskirts, he received his first shock. There was a large housing estate – a grubby, depressed-looking housing estate. With rising anxiety, he motored on into the town. He had booked them rooms at the Palace Hotel, which he remembered as an endearingly grand Edwardian building facing the sea and the pier. Oh, that wonderful theatre at the end of the pier where his parents had taken him with his sister to watch vaudeville shows.

As he headed for the seafront, he saw that all the little shops that used to sell things like ice cream and postcards had been replaced by chain stores. The main street that ran parallel to the seafront had been widened and was full of traffic. He longed now to reach the genteel relaxation of the Palace. He edged through a snarl of traffic. On the front, the black-and-grey sea heaved angrily, sending up plumes of spray. There was the pier, but the part where the theatre had been had fallen into the sea.

He parked in front of the Palace and waited for someone to rush out and take their suitcases. No one appeared. There was a flashing neon sign at the side that said, 'ar ark', two of the necessary letters having rusted away. He drove in. Agatha was ominously silent. He heaved their cases out of the boot and began to trundle them round to the front of the hotel. A gust of rain met them as they emerged from the car park, and Agatha's carefully coiffed hair whipped about her face. Inside, the entrance lounge, once a haven of large armchairs and log fire and palm trees, was dotted about with fake leather chairs, and where the log fire had been was an electric heater.

James checked them in. In his youth, the staff had worn smart uniforms. But it was a languid, pallid girl with a nose stud who checked the reservations.

Separate rooms, thought Agatha. I might have known it. There was no porter, so James had to lug the suitcases into the lift. 'You're in room twenty,' he said brightly. 'Here's your key.' No modern plastic cards at the Palace. The only relic of the old days lay in the large brass key he handed to Agatha.

She took it from him silently and unlocked the door. James said, 'See you downstairs in about an hour.'

'Sure,' said Agatha. She wheeled her case into the room and shut the door on him.

She sat down on the bed and looked around. A massive mahogany wardrobe loomed over the room. There was a round table at the window covered with a faded lace cloth. The carpet, which had once been green and covered with red roses, had worn down to a uniform dull colour. There was a badly executed seascape on one wall. A reminder of the hotel's glory days was a marble fireplace, but the hearth had been sealed up and a two-bar electric heater squatted in front of it. Beside the fireplace was a meter box for coins. No mini bar. No free coffee or tea. Rain rattled against the window and the wind moaned like a banshee. The bed was covered in a slippery pink quilt, the forerunner of the duvet and the kind of covering guaranteed to slide off the bed on a cold night.

Agatha wondered what to do. Common sense told her to ring down for a taxi and get the hell out of Snoth-on-Sea. Fantasy told her that the weather might change and the sun might shine and James and she would get married again.

Fantasy won.

But the one bit of common sense left urged her to get some warm clothes. In the main street, she had noticed a shop that sold country wear. Glad

21

that she had worn a coat for the journey, she went downstairs. At least they had some umbrellas for guests in a stand by the door. She took one and battled against the wind round the corner and into the main street. In the shop, she bought warm trousers and socks, a green Barbour coat and a rain hat. Then she went into a department store next door and bought several pairs of plain white knickers to replace the sexy flimsy things she had brought with her, and a cheap pair of serviceable walking shoes.

She carried her purchases back to the hotel and changed into a sweater and trousers, warm socks and the walking shoes, and went down to the bar.

James was sitting at a table in the corner of the bar, looking out at the heaving sea. Piped music was playing in the bar. Agatha sat down opposite him and said, 'I would like a stiff gin and tonic.'

James signalled to a waitress, who took the order with a look on her pasty face as if he had just insulted her. When her drink arrived – no ice and a tired bit of lemon – Agatha took a fortifying swig and opened her mouth to blast him.

But he disarmed her by saying ruefully, 'I've made a dreadful mistake. I'm sorry. It used to be a magical place for me. It was so quiet and peaceful. This hotel used to be so grand with an orchestra playing in the evenings. Look at it now! Because I came here as a child, I suppose I only remembered the sunny days. I'll make it up to you. We'll only stay a couple of days and then we'll move on somewhere. Go to Dover and take the ferry to France. Something like that.

'I checked the dinner menu. It seems pretty good. We'll have another drink and go into the dining room. I'm hungry. You?'

Agatha smiled at him fondly. 'I would love something to eat.'

The dining room was cavernous and cold. The chandeliers of James's youth had been replaced by harsh lighting. There were very few guests. A large table at the window was occupied by a family, or what Agatha judged to be a family. A plump woman with dyed blonde hair and a fat face had a harsh grating voice that carried across the dining room. Beside her was a small, crushed-looking man in a suit, collar and tie. He kept fiddling with his tie as if longing to take it off. A young woman dressed in black leather was poking at her food and occasionally talking to a young man with a shaven head and tattoos on the back of his hands. An older man with neat hair and a little Hitler moustache was smiling indulgently all around. His companion was very thin, with flaming red hair and green eye shadow.

The woman with the fat face caught Agatha staring at them and shouted across the dining room, 'Hey, you there! Mind yer own business, you silly cow.'

James half rose to his feet, but Agatha was already out of her chair and across the room to confront the woman.

'You just shut your stupid face and let me get on with my meal,' hissed Agatha.

'Shove off, you old trout.'

'Screw you,' said Agatha viciously and stalked back to join James.

'Remember Wyckhadden?' asked Agatha. 'It was a lovely place compared to this.'

'I would rather forget Wyckhadden,' said James coldly. Agatha blushed. Although she had been working on a murder case there, she had forgotten that James had found her in bed with Charles in Wyckhadden.

They had both ordered lobster bisque to start. It was white, lumpy and tasteless.

'I want a word with you.'

The shaven-headed man was looming over them. 'This is mum's honeymoon and you in-sulted her.'

'She started it,' protested Agatha.

'Look, just go away,' said James.

'Think you're the big shot,' sneered Shaven Head. 'Come outside.'

'Don't be silly.'

'Come outside or I'll shove your face in here.'

James sighed and threw down his napkin and followed Shaven Head from the dining room.

'That's the stuff!' jeered Fat Face.

'If you harm one hair of his head,' shouted Agatha, 'I'll murder you, you rotten bitch.'

The manager hurried into the dining room. 'What's all this noise? What's going on here?'

'Nothing,' said Fat Face.

Agatha hurried out of the dining room. James

was just coming back into the hotel. 'The rain's stopped,' he said mildly.

'Are you hurt?'

'Not as much as the other fellow.'

They returned to their table. Shaven Head limped in nursing a fat lip. The family at the round table talked in urgent whispers, throwing venomous glances at Agatha and James.

The next course was chicken à la Provençal. It was rubbery chicken covered in tinned tomatoes.

Agatha threw down her fork in disgust. 'James, let's get out of here and find a pub or a fish and chip shop.'

'You wait here,' said James. 'I'm going to have a word with the manager first. I'm not a snob, but that family from hell should never have been allowed to stay here. They're terrorizing the other guests.'

'In all the row, I didn't notice the other guests.'

Agatha turned round. An elderly couple were eating as fast as they could, no doubt wanting to make a quick escape. A young couple with a small child had their heads bent so low over their plates, they looked as if they wished they could disappear into them.

'I'm not staying here with the family from hell,' said Agatha. 'I'm coming with you!'

Chapter Two

The manager, Mr Beeston, led them into his office and shut the door. 'I'm so sorry about all this,' he said. He was a small round man wearing a dark jacket and pinstriped trousers. 'They wrote to book the honeymoon suite for Mr and Mrs Jankers, and a room for her son, Wayne Weldon, and his wife, Chelsea.'

'Who are the other couple?' asked James. 'The woman with the red hair and her husband?'

'That's Mr Cyril Hammond and his wife, Dawn. Friends of the family, I think. It all sounded very respectable. Times are hard and I was glad of the bookings. Then last night they started making trouble for the other guests and also for the townspeople who use the bar. I ordered them to leave and they refused. I called the police and they said they couldn't do anything about it. There had been no actual violence, you see.'

'There has been now,' James pointed out. 'Wayne tried to punch my head in.'

'Look, they are leaving the day after tomorrow.'

'I doubt we can last that long,' said James. 'I

used to come here as a child when it was a little seaside village and this was a grand hotel.'

'Must have been ages ago,' said the manager.

'The food's awful,' complained Agatha.

'That's the new cook. He came with good references. I was so desperate I didn't check them. It's all getting me down.'

Mr Beeston smelt strongly of whisky.

'Let me see,' said James. 'This is Saturday. We'll stay until Monday. I've got to make travel arrangements. Come along, Agatha. We'll find something to eat.'

'There's a great old pub along here,' said James, shouting against the gale. 'The Green Man. My parents used to rave about it.'

He turned up one of the narrow lanes that led away from the seafront. The Green Man was still there. 'Come on, Agatha. You're going to love this place.'

James pushed open the door and ushered Agatha in. Then he stood behind her, blinking in dismay. What had once been three bars, lounge, private and public, had been knocked into one large room. Music was blaring out. On a raised platform at the end of the room, a girl wearing nothing but a G-string undulated round a pole to the cheers and leers of crowds of white, pasty-faced youth.

They backed out into the rain. 'When I was in the main street buying warm clothes,' said Agatha, 'I saw an Indian restaurant.'

'Won't do,' said James sadly. 'Nothing the British drunk loves more than a curry.'

'And a Chinese.'

'We'll try the Chinese.'

To their relief the Chinese restaurant only contained a few quiet couples. Agatha took off her coat and then exclaimed, 'I've lost my scarf. I must have dropped it in the dining room.'

'We'll get it when we go back. Let's order.'

Put in a good mood by what turned out to be an excellent meal, they discussed travel plans, Agatha at last agreeing to James's suggestion that they should take the ferry to France and motor down to the Mediterranean.

Outside her hotel room, Agatha hesitated slightly, wondering whether to invite James in, and then decided against it. Let any romance wait until the sunny beaches of the Mediterranean.

The sun shone the next day, but that only made the town look shabbier. James trudged around various places he remembered from his youth, only to find they had been built over or had changed for the worse. Even the wide sandy beach had been eroded by the rising seas and was now only a thin strip of shingle at the bottom of the sea wall. Every high tide, waves crashed over the wall, sending huge plumes of spray like ghostly arms towards the houses and hotel. James thought that unless they built a proper barrier, it would not be long before the sea engulfed the front of the town.

'What's causing it?' asked Agatha. 'Melting ice caps? But it's so cold for June. Where's all this global warming?'

'Don't worry. We'll be off to the sunshine tomorrow. Did you find your scarf?'

'No. The manager said no one had handed it in. Maybe I was wearing it and it blew away.'

Agatha felt they were walking and talking like two bachelors. She cheered herself with the thought of balmy evenings on the Mediterranean. They drove over to Brighton that evening and had an excellent meal.

By the following morning, Agatha was in high spirits as they said goodbye to Snoth-on-Sea. It'll be a cold day in hell before I ever return to this dump, she told herself.

They were approaching Dover when James suddenly said, 'I'd better pull over. There's a police car racing along behind us.' He drew to the side of the road. To their amazement, the police car stopped in front of them. Then another police car coming out of Dover joined them.

James let down the window as two policemen and a man in plain clothes approached the car. The plain-clothes man flashed a badge and asked, 'Are you Mr James Lacey and Mrs Agatha Raisin?'

'Yes,' said James. 'But look here –'

'Get out of the car. Both of you. We don't want any trouble.'

Bewildered, they got out and stood in the sunshine. Cars slowed down as they passed; curious eyes stared from car windows.

'I am Detective Inspector Barret of the Snoth-on-Sea CID,' said the plain-clothes man. 'Mrs Raisin, we are taking you in for questioning over the murder of Geraldine Jankers . . .'

'What!' screeched Agatha.

Agatha was taken off in a police car. James followed, driving his own car and accompanied by a policeman.

The police station at Snoth-on-Sea was a Victorian one. Cameras went off in Agatha's face as she was ushered in. She shouted over her shoulder at James, 'Get a lawyer.'

The police station smelt of urine, disinfectant and strong tea. Agatha was led to an interview room and locked in. She sat at a scarred table. The only light was from a barred window, which looked as if it had not been cleaned since the police station had been built.

Agatha was later to regret that she had not waited for the arrival of the lawyer before she was questioned. She was so confident that it was all a silly mistake and angry at the interruption of her journey with James that she decided to adopt a lofty tone.

After ten minutes the door opened and the arresting detectives entered. A tape was put in. Inspector Barret and a Detective Sergeant Wilkins began the questioning. Agatha agreed that, yes, she was Mrs Agatha Raisin and added that she ran her own detective agency.

Barret pushed a plastic evidence bag across the table. 'Do you recognize this scarf?'

'Yes, it's mine,' said Agatha. 'I lost it.'

'When exactly did you lose it?'

'I don't know. The night before last, maybe. Look, what is all this about?'

'I explained when I took you in for questioning,' said Barret.

'I was too shocked and angry to listen to you. Explain again.'

'You are being questioned about the murder of Geraldine Jankers.'

'That fat bitch at the hotel?'

'You were heard threatening to murder her.'

'Oh, you silly man,' said Agatha contemptuously, 'a lot of people threaten to murder people when they get angry. I still don't see what this has to do with me.'

'You have identified your scarf. Mrs Jankers was found dead on the beach. She had been strangled with your scarf.'

Agatha looked at him in horror. He stared back with a look of dislike on his normally impassive face. He was a thickset man in need of a new suit because the grey one he was wearing was stretched at the seams. He had a heavy, open-pored face with shaggy eyebrows over grey eyes. His sergeant was younger, with a narrow face, pointed nose and long thin mouth. Agatha realized in that moment that she should have waited for a lawyer. She had badly antagonized both of them. But in the hope of remedying the situation, she smiled and said, 'Anyone could have used my scarf.'

'But you were the only one overheard threatening to murder her. Now describe your movements since arriving in Snoth-on-Sea.'

So in a subdued voice, Agatha did.

'You and Mr Lacey had separate rooms at the hotel. What is your relationship with Mr Lacey?'

'He is my ex-husband. We were about to go on holiday together.'

'Leaving the country?'

'Yes, but –'

The door opened and a policewoman said, 'Mrs Raisin's lawyer is here.'

A well-dressed, elegant man entered the room. 'If you do not mind, gentlemen, I would like a word with my client.'

Barret told the tape that he was ending the interview and then switched it off. He and Wilkins left the room.

'I am Jeremy Posselthwaite,' said the lawyer. 'I am an old friend of James Lacey. He called me on my mobile and it was fortunate I just happened to be in Brighton at the time. What have they got on you?'

'This dead woman insulted me in the dining room of the hotel. I said something about wanting to murder her. I lost my scarf. She was evidently found strangled with it. That's it.'

'And before you came here, you had never met Mrs Jankers before?'

'Never.'

'I gather from James that they not only insulted you and the other hotel guests but that Wayne Weldon, the son, picked a fight with James and came off badly.'

'Yes.'

'They are still trying to estimate the time of death. They guess she was murdered sometime last night. Where were you?'

'We were in Brighton. We wanted some decent food, so we went to a French restaurant called Le Village. It's in the Lanes.'

'And when did you return to the hotel?'

'About eleven in the evening. Look, this Mrs Jankers was found dead on the beach. She detested me as much as I detested her, although we had only met in the dining room the evening before. How on earth could I be able to persuade her to take a walk on the beach with me?'

'When did you find your scarf was missing?'

'It was after we left the dining room on our first evening. We couldn't stand the food, so we went to a Chinese restaurant. That was when I discovered the scarf was missing and I thought I must have left it in the dining room.'

'Perhaps Mrs Jankers took it. Or whoever murdered her. They haven't formally charged you with anything, have they?'

'No, all they are doing is questioning me.'

'Well, the first thing to do is to get you out of here. If they have further questions, they can check with you at your hotel. They really haven't got much to hold you on. Back in a minute.'

An hour later Agatha and James walked gloomily along the seafront. They had been told not to leave the town.

'Oh, look,' said Agatha, 'even the seagulls are dirty. Why is that, do you think? There doesn't seem to be much industry around here.'

'Bugger the seagulls,' said James moodily. 'What are we going to do?'

'I think I'll ask Patrick and Harry to come down here and help us solve this case.'

'Let's leave it to the police for once.'

'No, I want out of here. Just think. Harry could put on that gothic look of his, or whatever it's supposed to be – you know, the studs and black leather – and get cosy with the Jankers family and friends. Patrick can work with us. The police always take to Patrick because he used to be one of theirs.'

They had reached a dusty bandstand at the edge of the promenade. 'Look at that,' said James. 'That bandstand used to glitter green and gold and the band played such jolly tunes.'

Agatha glanced sideways at him and realized for the first time that she neither knew nor understood James. The clouds of obsession were clearing away, leaving her looking at a stranger.

They walked up into the bandstand. Litter blew around their feet.

James stood silently, looking out to sea. I never

thought he might be an unhappy man, thought Agatha. Surely only an unhappy man would chase after fond memories of childhood.

She took out her mobile phone. 'Look, James. I'm going to phone them at the office and then we'll get something to eat, but not at the hotel.'

He did not reply, so she shrugged and phoned Mrs Freedman and asked to speak to Patrick.

'Hello,' said Patrick. 'I'm afraid things here are still quiet. Where are you phoning from?'

'A dreary dump called Snoth-on-Sea. Let me tell you what's been happening here.'

Agatha briskly outlined their supposed involvement in the murder of Mrs Jankers. 'I want you and Harry to come down here and help me solve this murder. Can Phil cope on his own?'

'I should think so, if we aren't away too long.'

'Can you both set out as quickly as possible? I'll book rooms for you at the hotel. No, on second thoughts, I'll book your room, Patrick. Tell Harry to book his own and to wear his skinhead black-leather look. I want him to cosy up to the dead woman's family.'

'We should both be down there by evening. Food good?'

'Lousy.'

'Okay, we'll eat on the road.'

Agatha felt more cheerful when she had rung off. 'Harry and Patrick will be here this evening,' she said.

'If you think that will do any good.' James had his shoulders hunched before the increasing wind.

35

'Well, it's better than mooning around here looking for your lost youth,' snapped Agatha.

'You really are a bitch.'

'I know,' said Agatha. 'Let's eat.'

After a moderately good pub lunch, they made their way back to the hotel. The manager greeted them with the news that Mr Cyril Hammond, the Jankerses' family friend, wished to speak to them and was waiting in the bar.

James remembered the bar as having once been an elegant place with white-coated waiters moving around among the palms. Now it was dingy. The long mahogany bar had been replaced by a plastic fake-wood one and the beautiful Victorian mirrors were gone. Low coffee tables had replaced the good old sturdy ones. 'Probably sold off the contents to an antique dealer,' said James. 'Oh, there's Hammond, over there by the window.'

Cyril Hammond rose to meet them. He had a sallow face and black hair combed straight back from his forehead. His little toothbrush moustache was neatly trimmed over a small thin mouth. He was wearing a dark blue blazer and white trousers with knife-edged pleats.

'Drink?' he asked.

He signalled to the solitary fat waitress, who lumbered up and took their orders, sighing heavily as she did so, as if overworked, although they were the only customers in the bar.

'I'm sorry about the incident,' said Cyril.

'Murder is hardly an incident,' Agatha pointed out.

'Oh, that. I meant Wayne picking a fight.'

'Why did you want to see us?' asked James. He took a sip of his cloudy half-pint of beer, made a face, and put it down on the table.

'It's like this. That detective, Barret, he said you, Mrs Raisin, were a private detective.'

He did not tell Agatha that Barret had added a bitter complaint that any weirdo these days could go around calling themselves a private detective.

'I am very successful,' said Agatha.

'I'm worried about the family and I want this cleared up. None of us would have touched her.'

'What about her husband? She was on her honeymoon?'

'Oh, Fred? I can't imagine him strangling anyone or having the strength to do it. It must have been some stranger.'

'The police don't know exactly when she was murdered,' said Agatha. 'Has anyone any idea why she went out walking on the beach? It's a peculiar place to go. I mean, there's hardly any beach left.' As if to illustrate her point, spray dashed against the windows.

'High tide,' commented Cyril. 'We don't know why Geraldine went out. Her husband says he was fast asleep and didn't hear her leave.'

'There are houses on either side of this hotel,' said James. 'Surely the police have been questioning people.'

'As far as I can gather,' said Cyril, 'nobody saw

anything. There are stairs down to the beach right opposite the hotel. Once down there, she couldn't be seen because of the promenade wall.'

'Do you want us to try to find out who did it?' asked Agatha.

'I wish you would. I don't have that much money . . .'

'It's all right,' said Agatha grandly. 'I'll be working for myself. I want to get out of this place as soon as possible.'

'Was Mrs Jankers married before?' asked James.

'Yes, three times.'

Agatha blinked in surprise. She thought she would never understand men. She had known attractive women who couldn't even get married once.

'How did the marriages end?' James asked.

'The first one – that would be Jimmy Weldon. He died of a heart attack. Then the second, Charlie Black, is doing time for armed robbery. She divorced him when he was in prison. Before Fred, there was Archie Swale. She divorced him before she met Fred at ballroom dancing classes.'

'It could be that this Archie Swale was bitter about the divorce. Do you know where he lives?'

'Brighton, last I heard.'

'You wouldn't happen to know his address?'

'I remember it was some house in Medlow Square. Can't recall the number.'

Agatha made a note.

'How long have you known Mrs Jankers?'

'A long time. We were kids together down the East End of London. Somehow we managed to keep in touch over the years. Geraldine was great fun.'

'Then why,' said Agatha, 'did she give me the distinct impression of being a noisy slag?'

'Poor Geraldine was having a bad menopause. She was never like that before.'

'Mr Hammond –'

'Call me Cyril.'

'Very well, Cyril it is,' said Agatha. 'Do you think you could persuade Wayne to speak to us?'

'Might be difficult. He's all broken up about his mother's death, but I'll try.'

Half an hour later, feeling they had extracted as much information as they could from Cyril, Agatha and James set out for Brighton to see if they could interview the ex-husband, Archie Swale.

They had bought a map of Brighton. Medlow Square came as a surprise to Agatha. It was a small square of trim Georgian houses. How had Geraldine managed to snare a husband who lived in such elegant surroundings?

After knocking at several doors, they learned that Archie lived at number ten.

'Let's hope he's at home,' said James, ringing the doorbell.

The door was answered by an elderly grey-haired man. His faded blue eyes looked at them from under heavy grey eyebrows. His face was criss-crossed by broken veins.

'We're looking for a Mr Archie Swale,' said Agatha.

'That's me. What do you want?'

'I am a private detective investigating the death of Geraldine Jankers,' said Agatha, wondering furiously just how old Archie was. Geraldine had been in her fifties. Archie looked to be somewhere in his eighties.

'I had nothing to do with the old bitch,' said Archie. The door began to close.

'We know you had nothing to do with it,' said James quickly. 'But we would like to know what sort of woman Geraldine was. That might give us a clue as to who murdered her.'

He studied them for a few moments and then shrugged. 'You'd better come in.'

He ushered them in and shut the door. Then he led the way into a living room on the ground floor. It was sparsely furnished with a few good pieces. Persian rugs lay on the floor. Above the marble fireplace was a very good seascape.

Agatha tried to imagine the blowsy Geraldine in such surroundings, and failed.

Agatha and James sat down on a sofa piled with silk-covered cushions faded with age. Archie took a seat in an armchair next to the fireplace.

'How long were you married?' asked Agatha.

'About a year.'

'Where did you meet her?'

'In a pub in Brighton. She was down from London for the day.'

'And what attracted you to her?'

'I was pretty lonely. My wife died fifteen years ago. Geraldine came up to my table and asked if she could join me, as all the other tables were taken. She seemed an easy, friendly sort.'

'Have you any photographs of her as she was then?'

He rose stiffly and went to a bureau by the window, opened a drawer and took out a photograph. He handed it to Agatha. 'That was us on our wedding day. Brighton Registry Office.'

Agatha stared at the photograph in surprise. Geraldine was slimmer and had brown hair.

'She was blonde when we saw her,' said Agatha, 'and fatter.'

'That was the thing,' he said. 'Soon as we were married, she started to change. I'd never met that son of hers before we were married and he came to stay with his wife. Scum they were. Wayne stole a gold cigarette case that had been my father's. I know he stole it, but Geraldine screamed at me for insulting her precious son. After that, things began to go rapidly downhill. She had seemed a nice, quiet lady before we were married. She liked her drink, but so do I. But she dyed her hair blonde and began to stay out late and wouldn't tell me where she had been. I thought I was trapped for life when she suddenly asked me for a divorce. I thought she would take me for every penny I had left, but she settled for an amicable divorce. I felt I had got off lightly.

'I heard she'd married again. It was on the

41

radio when they were announcing the murder. What can I tell you about her? I think she was a bit of an actress. I mean, the difference before our wedding and after was astounding. I inherited this house from an aunt. I now live on my pension. I think the fact that I wasn't well off upset her. She had a nasty mouth on her. I began to be frightened of her.'

'Did you know she had been married twice before you?' asked James.

'Yes, she said they had both died.'

'The first one did. The other is doing time for armed robbery.'

They continued to question him for the next quarter of an hour, but Archie did not have much more to tell them and so they left.

'Let's go back and brief Patrick and try to have a quiet word with Harry,' said Agatha. 'I wonder whether that armed robber ex of hers is still in prison.'

Chapter Three

Patrick was sitting in the hotel bar when they arrived. Agatha often wished he would dress more casually. From his neatly combed grey hair and lugubrious face to his suit, collar and tie and well-polished black shoes, he seemed to scream cop.

They sat down and ordered drinks and then began to tell him the whole story of what they had found out so far in detail. 'So what we want you to do for a start,' said Agatha finally, 'is to use your police contacts and find out if Geraldine's second husband, Charlie Black, is still doing time in prison.'

'I'll try,' said Patrick.

'Where's Harry?'

'He went out for a look around the town.'

'Does he look the part?'

'Oh, God, yes. He even followed me down on his motorbike. Black leather, shaved head, tattoos, studs, the lot.'

'Do you know what room he's in?'

'Two five seven.'

'We'll call on him later when the coast is clear.'

'Excuse me.'

They looked round and saw Cyril Hammond. 'I can't get Wayne to speak to you, but Fred Jankers said he would like a word. He wants to see you in his room.'

'Now?' asked James.

'If you wouldn't mind.'

Patrick said he would go round to the police station to make friends with the local force. Agatha and James followed Cyril. Cyril was now wearing a yachting cap.

'Would it be possible,' said Agatha to Cyril's back, 'to have a word with your wife?'

That back stiffened noticeably. He turned round. 'I don't know if she can tell you anything that I don't know.'

Agatha looked at him silently. 'Oh, very well,' he said reluctantly. 'When you're finished with Fred, I'll bring Dawn down to the bar.'

'We would really like to talk to your wife on her own,' said James.

'Why?'

'Wives often find the presence of a husband a bit intimidating.'

As if you would know anything about marriage, thought Agatha bitterly.

'All right,' said Cyril with obvious reluctance.

He walked on and they followed him along one of the hotel's long corridors. He stopped at a door and shouted, 'It's me, Cyril.'

A faint voice answered and he opened the door and went in, followed by Agatha and James.

Fred Jankers was sitting in a chair by the

44

window. He was a small man with black hair, which looked as if it had been dyed, combed in sparse lines across his head. He had a small face and small black eyes.

He was wearing a charcoal-grey suit which hung about him in folds, a striped shirt and a black silk tie.

'Sit down,' said Fred. His room faced the sea. They could hear the waves pounding the sea wall.

Agatha and James found two hard chairs and Cyril sat on the bed.

'I want you to find out who killed my Geraldine,' said Fred. His voice was high and reedy.

'We'll do our best,' said James and Agatha threw him an irritated look. After all, *she* was the detective.

'We'd like to know as much as you can tell us about your late wife,' said Agatha. 'Where did you meet her?'

'Ballroom dancing class. I was a bit shy, but she latched on to me right away.'

'What is your job or profession?'

'I own a chain of small dress shops. I think that's what attracted Geraldine to me. She was very fashion-conscious.'

Like hell she was, thought Agatha, remembering Geraldine's blowsy appearance; it was your money she was after.

'Do you inherit your wife's money?' she asked.

'No, she left it all to her son, Wayne. I only found that out this morning when I phoned the solicitor.'

'I suppose she hadn't had time to change her will,' put in James.

'That must be it. Geraldine was devoted to me.'

'Now, the night of the murder,' said Agatha, 'you went to sleep as usual. What time was this?'

'About eleven o'clock in the evening. She was pacing up and down the room. I said, "Come to bed. This isn't much of a honeymoon." She said, "Go to sleep. I've got to think." I slept all night and when I awoke, I saw her bed wasn't slept in and then the police arrived.'

'They found my scarf round her neck. I lost it. Did she pick it up?'

Fred looked uncomfortable. 'It was lying on the dining room floor. Yes, she said something about finders, keepers.'

'Did you tell the police this?'

'I didn't like to. I wanted to protect her memory. I didn't want the police to think of her as a thief.'

'You'd better tell them now. You could have saved me from enduring hours of questioning. Did she receive a phone call?'

'No, not that I know of.'

'Have you a photo of your wedding day?' asked James.

'Yes, I have one with me.' Fred pulled out his wallet and extracted a square photograph. There was Geraldine, slimmer, looking demure in a blue silk tailored suit and a little blue hat with an eye veil.

James handed back the photograph. 'Immediately after you were married, did she change? When was the wedding?'

'Four weeks ago. We decided to delay the honeymoon because I had a lot of business to attend to. Did she change? She ate an awful lot and put on weight. Apart from that, she was pretty much the same.'

'Why Snoth-on-Sea?' asked Agatha.

'Geraldine came here as a kid. She said she and her parents were staying at a bed and breakfast. She said the Palace Hotel was ever so posh and she always dreamed of staying there.'

'Did you know that her second husband was in jail for armed robbery?'

'No!' He looked amazed. 'You see, it was a whirlwind romance.' He gave a reminiscent smile. 'She swept me off my feet. We were married a few weeks after I met her. I didn't have much time to find out who she knew. I didn't even know she had a son and daughter-in-law until she told me they would be coming on the honeymoon, along with her friend, Cyril, and his wife.'

'Didn't you object?'

He shifted uneasily in his chair. 'I did say something, but she said we would have the rest of our lives together. Then I found out I had to pay for everyone and I wasn't too pleased. But she hugged me and said, "You can afford it, darling, and it would make me so happy."'

Agatha wondered what Geraldine had actually

said. The foul-mouthed woman had probably bullied the meek Fred into it.

'So you can't think of anyone who would want to kill her?'

'Why would anyone?' Fred raised his eyes to the ceiling. 'As God is my witness, she hadn't an enemy in the world.'

She made me one in two seconds flat, thought Agatha.

Neither Agatha nor James could think of anything else to ask him. Fred thanked them and again said he hoped they could find out who had murdered his wife.

As they walked downstairs, James said, 'Well, that was odd. He doesn't seem entirely broken up, does he?'

'Grief takes people in odd ways,' said Agatha. 'But no, he did seem unnaturally calm about the whole thing. And he phoned the solicitor. I wonder how much Geraldine was worth.'

Cyril Hammond and his wife, Dawn, were waiting in the bar. 'Poor Fred,' said Cyril. 'How's he taking it?'

'Seems to be bearing up pretty well,' commented Agatha. 'Now may we have a word with Mrs Hammond on her own?'

Cyril looked about to protest, but then said, 'Okay, I'll be up in my room.'

Agatha and James sat down with Dawn. Her hair was an even more ferocious colour of red th~n when Agatha had first seen her, and she   unnaturally thin, with deep shadows under   es and arms like sticks.

'What about a drink?' she asked in a throaty voice.

James signalled to the waitress. 'What would you like?'

'Vodka and Red Bull.'

James ordered what she wanted, gin and tonic for Agatha and a bottle of beer for himself.

'We are trying to get a picture of what Mrs Jankers was like,' began Agatha.

'Why? You saw her.'

'I mean her personality, her friends, anyone she was frightened of.'

The drinks arrived. Dawn took a swig of hers and then said, 'People were frightened of Geraldine, not the other way round. Me, I didn't want to come on this bleeding honeymoon, but Cyril, he says that Geraldine had pleaded with him to come along. Now, take my word for it, dear Geraldine never pleaded with anyone. But Cyril always had a soft spot for her. You want to know what she was like? A great fat spider, that's what. Always on the lookout for a fellow with money. Before she married Fred, she was as meek as anything. After they were married, she reverted to her usual shit-mouthed self. I said to Cyril that this whole honeymoon was sick, sick, sick.'

'Did you know that her second husband was doing time for armed robbery?'

'Charlie, oh, sure. I knew Charlie. The only thing I liked about that villain was that he knew how to shut Geraldine up. Smacked her across the mouth once.'

49

'Who did he rob?'

'Some jeweller in Lewisham. They got him, but they never found the jewels.'

'Is he still in prison?'

'As far as I know.'

'Who would have wanted to kill Geraldine?'

'Just about everyone I can think of.'

'Her husband?'

'Fred? Naw. Poor little bugger got sandbagged by her. He's not exactly weeping over her death. But Fred couldn't hurt anyone.'

'What about her son?'

'Wayne? Her own son! Why?'

'He inherits.'

'Don't think she would leave enough to make her own son murder her.'

'Did you know that Geraldine stole my scarf, the one she was found strangled with?'

'Who told you that?'

'Mr Jankers. He said she found it lying in the dining room after we had left.'

'Now there's a thing. He left us thinking you must have murdered her.'

James interrupted. 'As to that, Agatha, I really think we should go along to the police station and tell them. With us in the clear, we can get out of here.'

But after they had said goodbye to Dawn and were walking along in the direction of the police station, Agatha began to fret. Only a short time ago, she had longed to get out of this terrible place and head south to the Mediterranean with James. She tried to conjure up a dream of James holding her in his arms on a hotel balcony overlooking the moonlit sea, but the dream would not come. They would probably have separate rooms, she thought wearily, and no doubt James would run into some old friends and she would be left on the outskirts of some party while they all chattered on about people she did not know.

At the police station, they asked to see Detective Inspector Barret. They were told to wait. Agatha sat down on a bench and suddenly wished she could smoke. She had been trying to cut down, but all the terrible threats about what happened to the health of smokers only made her want to smoke more.

'Cheer up, Agatha,' said James. 'We'll soon be heading south.'

'I don't –' Agatha was just beginning when they were told that Barret would see them. They were taken to an interview room.

James gave Agatha a puzzled look. 'You were starting to say something.'

But at that moment Barret walked in.

He listened in silence as Agatha told him about Mr Jankers's confession that his wife had actually found Agatha's scarf where she had dropped it in the dining room.

'We'll need to take another statement from him,' said Barret. 'Why didn't he tell us in the first place?'

'He didn't want to sully his wife's good name.'

51

'I'll be having a sharp word with him. Wasting police time unnecessarily. Sending us off chasing after you two.'

'When you get your statement,' asked James, 'will we be free to leave?'

'Yes, I see no reason to keep you.'

Agatha was unnaturally silent when they left the police station.

'Well, that's that,' said James at last. 'We can pack up and be on our way.'

'Don't you want to find out who murdered Geraldine?'

'I neither know nor care.'

'But I've brought Harry and Patrick down. Think of the expense.'

'That's your fault. You haven't charged anyone anything.'

'But think of the good publicity if I solve the case. Besides, I was photographed going into the police station and photos appeared in the papers with captions giving my name and saying I was helping the police with their inquiries, which made me look guilty.'

James stopped abruptly. 'Agatha, I do not want to stay in this place a moment longer than I have to. If you won't come with me – well, I'll just go on my own. I could do with a decent holiday after this.'

Agatha stared up at him, the wind from the sea blowing her jacket about her stocky figure, her eyes narrowing.

'I can't just leave it,' she said stubbornly.

James looked back at her with something like amazement in his blue eyes. Where had the Agatha gone who would have gone through fire and water to be with him?

'I think you are being selfish and silly,' he said flatly.

'No, it's you who are being selfish. It was selfish in the extreme to pick out this place for a holiday simply because you wanted to wander down memory lane.'

'I have nothing more to say to you,' said James haughtily.

He stalked off. Agatha watched him go. As he approached the hotel, a large wave burst over the sea wall and drenched him from head to foot.

'There is a God,' said Agatha Raisin.

She realized when she got to the hotel that she was very hungry. Somewhere deep inside her was an ache because of James's behaviour. Agatha went to Harry's room and tapped on the door.

Harry opened it. The odour of fish and chips wafted out of the room.

'Got any of that fish supper left?' asked Agatha.

'Just about to start. Come in. We can share it.'

'Have you met Wayne Weldon and his equally terrible wife?' said Agatha, walking into the room.

'Not yet. I was just taking a recce round the

53

town. Horrible little place. I'll be down there at breakfast time and strike up a conversation. Dig in, Agatha. Loads of fish and chips.'

'No knives and forks?'

'Course not.'

'Anything to drink?'

'I've got a bottle of wine. I'll get another glass out of the bathroom.'

They ate and drank in silence. Then Agatha told Harry all she had found out.

'Hasn't been much of a second honeymoon for you, has it?' commented Harry.

'It wasn't a second honeymoon,' said Agatha defiantly. 'James is leaving tomorrow to holiday on his own.' Then, to Agatha's horror, she gave a gulping sob and began to cry.

'Here, now,' said Harry, moving his chair next to hers and giving her a hug. 'The man's a bastard. You're better off without him.'

He handed Agatha a clean handkerchief. Agatha blew her nose and gulped and then dried her eyes. 'You won't look the part,' she said, giving him a watery smile, 'if you're going to carry clean handkerchiefs about with you. Don't these studs hurt?'

Harry had one in his nose and one in his upper lip. 'No, but I wish I'd never started wearing them. I suppose I'll need to have surgery to get the holes filled up. So why is James leaving?'

'Like I told you, Fred Jankers had confessed to the fact that his wife found my scarf and kept it. We told the police and the police said we were free to go.'

'You've got me and Patrick here,' said Harry. 'Why don't you go off and have a nice holiday?'

Agatha sighed. 'Because horrible reality is creeping in and I don't think it would be a nice holiday at all.'

There was a knock at the door.

Harry walked over to it and called, 'Who's there?'

'Patrick,' came the reply.

Harry opened the door.

'I just saw James Lacey lugging his suitcase out of the hotel,' said Patrick. 'Where's he going?'

'On holiday,' said Agatha bleakly. 'By himself. I didn't know he meant to leave tonight.'

Harry flashed a warning look at Patrick.

Agatha caught that look. She knew Harry was trying to warn Patrick not to pursue the subject. How strange that young Harry, with his shaven head, leather and studs, should be so considerate. But, then, Harry in conventional dress could look quite attractive.

'To business,' said Agatha briskly, while deep inside her a little Agatha ran about, tearing her hair and weeping for lost love. 'Is Charlie Black out of prison?'

'Yes,' said Patrick. 'There's a copper along at the station, knew some friends of mine from the old days. He checked up for me. He got out two weeks ago.'

Agatha's eyes gleamed. 'Wait a bit. He robbed a jewellery store in Lewisham. The police got him, but they never got the jewels. Just say he left them with Geraldine. He arranges to meet her on the beach. He asks about the jewels. What if she says she sold them and spent the money? He strangles her in a rage.'

'Now, that's possible,' said Patrick. 'He appears to have had a history of violence.'

'I don't see it,' said Harry. 'If she had sold the jewels or still had them and had no intention of giving them to him, she wouldn't meet him on a deserted beach at dead of night. Come to think of it, the body must have been found pretty quickly. There's only a strip of shingle at low tide.'

'I found out,' said Patrick. 'She was spotted by a man walking his dog at one in the morning, and eleven-thirty in the evening was low tide. The shingle is only exposed for two hours, and when the police got to her, the sea had nearly reached the body. So they think she was murdered sometime between, say, eleven-thirty and one in the morning. They won't be completely sure until the full results of the autopsy are in.'

'Did you get the name of the man who saw her?'

'Chap called George Bonford. Lives along the promenade. Said his dog's getting old and, like old people, wants to pee the whole time, so he took him out. Dog stopped to pee. Bonford stopped and looked over the wall and saw her lying on the beach. He could see her body quite clearly in the street lights on the promenade.'

'So Harry's going to try to get to know Wayne and wife, and you, Patrick, are going to see the dog walker. I wonder what I should do. I know,

I think I'll get to know Cyril Hammond better. So that's all for tonight.'

Agatha lay in bed that night visualizing James speeding towards the Channel ferry. 'I've done the right thing,' she cried to the uncaring ceiling, 'so why does it hurt so much?'

James drove through the night, his mouth set in a firm line. He remembered he had friends who ran a bed and breakfast at their villa outside Marseilles. Suddenly his mouth relaxed in a smile. As soon as he could the next day, he would send Agatha a postcard with their address. He knew his Agatha. She wouldn't – couldn't – hold out.

She'd probably fly down to Marseilles and rent a car. She might even be there before him!

Ah, he knew his Agatha so well.

Back in Carsely the following morning, Sir Charles Fraith stood irresolute outside Agatha's cottage. He was a friend of hers who dropped in and out of her life when it suited him to do so. He had a key to the cottage, but as he stood there he knew there was no one inside. The house had that feel about it, even though Agatha's car was parked outside.

He decided to visit Mrs Bloxby at the vicarage.

Mrs Bloxby welcomed him with pleasure. She

liked Charles, always so well tailored and neat, from his expensively barbered fair hair to his handmade shoes.

'Coffee in the garden?' she asked. 'Such a fine day.'

'Lovely.'

Charles went through the French windows into the garden and sat down, enjoying the smell of flowers and the domestic sounds of clattering cups in the kitchen.

Mrs Bloxby reappeared carrying a laden tray. 'I've just made a batch of scones,' she said. 'Help yourself. I suppose you are wondering where Mrs Raisin is.'

'Yes, I phoned the office and Mrs Freedman only said she wasn't in today.'

'I am very worried about her. You see, James took her off on some mystery holiday.'

'Poor Agatha. The never-ending dream.'

'Well, Mrs Raisin, I am sure, was hoping for somewhere romantic, but I saw an item in the newspapers which worried me.'

'What's she been up to? I haven't been reading the papers.'

'I'll get it for you.'

Mrs Bloxby went into the house and came back with a cutting. It showed a photograph of Agatha and James arriving at the Snoth-on-Sea police station. The story underneath said that a Mrs Geraldine Jankers had been found dead on the beach and Mrs Agatha Raisin and Mr James Lacey were helping police with their inquiries.

'Snoth-on-Sea doesn't sound a romantic place,' said Charles.

'I am sure Mr Lacey had a romantic reason known only to himself for going there.'

'Murder does seem to follow Aggie around. I might go down there.'

'I do not think that is wise,' said Mrs Bloxby. 'Mr Lacey certainly would not welcome your presence.'

After he had left her, Charles drove home. He went on the Internet and looked up hotels in Snoth-on-Sea. There appeared to be only one main hotel. The Palace. He rang up the hotel and asked to speak to Agatha. He was told she was out. Charles had a sudden idea. He asked to speak to James Lacey. He was told Mr Lacey had checked out.

'Thought that pair would quarrel sooner rather than later,' he said. 'Oh, well, may as well pay Aggie a visit.'

Chapter Four

In the dining room the following morning, Harry spotted his quarry. Wayne and his wife, Chelsea, were sitting alone. Neither the Hammonds nor Fred Jankers had put in an appearance.

Harry also noticed an elderly couple and a thirtyish couple seated at tables. Had they been in the hotel at the time of the murder? Agatha had not mentioned being suspicious of other hotel guests.

He looked gloomily down at his greasy breakfast, wondering how to strike up a conversation with Wayne and Chelsea. Then he noticed they had a ketchup bottle on their table, whereas he had none.

He got to his feet and strolled over to them. 'Mind if I borrow your ketchup?' he asked. Wayne was even more unsavoury close up. His eyes were close together and his nose looked as if someone had squashed it. Chelsea had brown hair highlighted with streaks of blonde. Her head was an odd shape, as if it had been crushed in a press. It was very narrow. She was wearing false eyelashes and false nails. Her skin was sallow and there was a rash of little pimples on her chin. Her eyes were as green as contact lenses could make them. She was wearing a blouse with fringing and a layered skirt. Harry recognized it as a now out-of-date fashion, which had been, at the time, dubbed Pocahontas Gone Bad.

Wayne studied Harry from his shaven head to his expensive sneakers, and suddenly smiled. 'Help yourself, mate.'

'Ta.' Harry lifted the bottle. Then he said, 'I'm Harry. What are a trendy pair like you doing in a dump like this?'

''Sawful, ain't it?' drawled Chelsea. 'Wayne's mum was here on her honeymoon but she got murdered.'

'Go on!' said Harry.

'Look, bring your breakfast over here,' said Wayne, 'and we'll tell you about it.'

That was easy, thought Harry. He picked up his plate of food and his coffee cup and sauntered over to join them.

'You must be feeling wrecked,' he said sympathetically.

'I'm feeling furious,' said Wayne, 'cos I knows who done it.'

'Who?'

'Some cow who calls herself a detective. Agatha Raisin.'

'Have the police arrested her?' asked Harry.

'No, the old bat's still here, snooping around. Cyril, that's a friend of mum's, he says that mum stole that scarf when that Agatha female dropped it.'

'What's this about a scarf?'

'Mum was strangled with it. On the beach. Middle of the night.'

'Blimey!'

'So we're all stuck here in this crap hotel while the police piss about.'

'Have you spoken to this Raisin woman?'

'What's the point? She has this fellow with her. He socked me, just like that.'

'Why?'

'I dunno. Spite. Posh chap.'

'Say it wasn't this Agatha woman,' said Harry. 'Did your mum have any enemies?'

'Not a one. Why are you asking all these questions?'

'Sorry. But I mean, a murder . . . Tell you what, you two need cheering up and the food here's awful. What say I take you to an Indian for lunch?'

'Could do with a pint and a vindaloo,' said Wayne.

'That would be great.' Chelsea batted her eyelashes at Harry.

'I'll pick you up in the reception at twelve-thirty,' said Harry. 'See ya.'

He strolled off, leaving his greasy breakfast on their table.

Later that morning, Patrick tracked down the dog walker, George Bonford. George invited Patrick into his house on the seafront and offered him coffee. Spray rattled against the front windows of his living room.

'Aren't you worried about getting washed away?' asked Patrick.

'Yes. We've had residents' meetings at the town hall to complain, but they won't do anything.' George was an elderly man with a good shock of white hair above his wrinkled face. 'Fact is, this used to be such a lovely place. Quiet, genteel. Then they began building more and more houses and moving the welfare cases in. There used to be a pretty café on the front. Now it's an amusement arcade. The good old pubs have gone and now they're full of lap dancers and drugs. Lots of drugs and not enough police to cope with them. Have you seen the youth of this place? They go around like zombies.'

'Tell me how you spotted the dead woman,' asked Patrick.

'My dog, Queenie, began to bark like she wanted to go out. She's old now, like me, and I know what it is to have a weak bladder. Anyway, I don't sleep that much these days. I put Queenie on her leash and took her out to do her business. I remember thinking I was lucky the tide was out. One of these days I'm going to be washed away. Queenie stopped to pee and I don't know why, but I looked over the wall and down to the beach. That's when I saw her.'

'Did you see or hear anyone else?'

'I was too shocked to take much notice of anything else. I mean, I could see her lying there, not moving, but I couldn't make out that she'd been strangled. For all I knew, she could have collapsed with a heart attack. I went straight home and called an ambulance. I went out again when I saw the ambulance arriving. Then men went down to her. One took out his phone. The next thing I knew, the police had arrived as well.'

'What time was this?'

'Around about one in the morning. If anyone else had been down on the beach, I'd have heard them. It was quiet and anyone walking on that shingle would have made a noise.'

Agatha longed for the days when American filter coffee had been served in cafés. Now it was all espresso. She was seated with Cyril in the Friendly Nook, a café that seemed anything but friendly. Two pasty-faced youths were openly smoking pot, ignoring the glares from a table of three middle-aged women.

Cyril had jumped at the idea of accompanying Agatha for a coffee. His wife had been nowhere in sight. Agatha wished he would take off his ridiculous yachting cap. Cyril was having to ignore jeers from the pot-smoking youths of 'Where did you park yer boat?'

Agatha sighed and took out her phone and called the police station. 'There are two young men openly smoking pot in the Friendly Nook café,' she said. 'Yes, I know it's not a major crime, but they are upsetting the customers.'

The youths saw her phoning, muttered something, and got up and left hurriedly.

'I'll bet you the police don't even bother to come,' said Agatha. 'But at least that's got rid of them.'

To Agatha's relief, Cyril took off his ridiculous hat and placed it on a chair next to him.

'Where's your friend, Mr Lacey?' asked Cyril.

'He had business to attend to,' said Agatha curtly.

'I'm glad I've got you all to myself,' said Cyril. He stroked his little moustache. 'Fact is, Dawn hasn't much time for me these days.'

'Perhaps the murder has upset her.'

'No, she hated poor Geraldine and made no bones about it. "I'll kill you one day." That's what she used to shout.'

Agatha's eyes widened. 'You don't think your wife . . .?'

'No, Dawn's all mouth and no action.'

'Did you know that Mrs Jankers's second husband is now out of prison?'

Cyril looked alarmed. 'I hope he doesn't come near here. That man frightened me to death.

He even accused me of having an affair with Geraldine.'

'How awful,' said Agatha, wondering whether it might have been true. 'The police never recovered the jewels that Charlie Black stole. Do you think Mrs Jankers knew where they were hidden?'

'No, definitely not. She would have told me. You know something? I don't think you should worry any more about this murder. Now that Fred has told the police that Geraldine stole your scarf, you're free to go. I mean, what can you do that the police can't?'

'There is a very small police force here and they don't seem to have turned it over to some larger force. It is my job, after all.'

'Such an awful job for such a pretty woman,' said Cyril almost automatically, as if his thoughts were elsewhere.

Harry was glad he had had the foresight to draw out plenty of cash, not wanting to flash his credit cards.

Having firmly established that he was paying for the meal, Wayne and Chelsea ordered a great deal of food and pints of beer to wash it down.

They were so intent on eating that he couldn't get much conversation out of them, but when Wayne finally burped and leaned back in his chair, Harry said, 'Nice to get away from that awful hotel.'

Wayne's eyes narrowed as if suspecting Harry might be 'posh'. 'Used to better, are you?' he jeered.

'We're all used to better,' said Harry quickly. He noticed Chelsea was wearing a sparkling necklace. 'That's a pretty necklace,' he said.

'Not real diamonds.' Chelsea fingered the necklace. 'Wayne gave to it me for our first wedding anniversary.'

At that moment, a ray of sunshine shot through the dusty brown curtains at the windows of the restaurant and sparked fire from the necklace.

'It looks real,' said Harry. 'Mind if I have a look?'

'Go ahead.' Chelsea raised her skinny arms to unclasp the necklace. Wayne seized one of her arms and growled, 'Leave it.' Then to Harry, 'Wot you so interested in necklaces and things for? You a poofter?'

Harry shrugged. 'Doesn't matter.' He began to talk about football and Wayne gradually began to relax, although he seemed to think the whole of the English team was made up of 'wankers'.

Deciding that the way to get any information about the murder was to talk about anything else and let Wayne perhaps let slip a few interesting facts, Harry amiably discussed football players, so that by the time they left the restaurant, Wayne and Chelsea appeared to consider themselves his close friends.

Wayne and Chelsea went off for a walk and

Harry headed back to the hotel. Agatha was just walking through reception on the way out. Seeing that the girl at the desk wasn't paying any attention and that apart from himself and Agatha the reception area was deserted, he muttered quickly, 'Got something interesting.'

'Car park in five minutes,' whispered Agatha. 'Blue Ford Escort.'

Harry slumped down in a chair and picked up a copy of the local paper. When he was sure the five minutes were up, he strolled round to the car park. A couple were getting into their car near where Agatha was parked, so he went over to his motorbike and pretended to examine it until they had driven off.

'Into the back seat and keep your head down,' said Agatha. 'I'll drive us somewhere quiet.'

Agatha had rented the car after having parted from Cyril. She drove up into the downs until she saw a pub called the Feathers standing on its own at a crossroads.

Harry, who had been lying down on the back seat, eased himself out of the car. 'I think this place is far enough away,' said Agatha.

They walked into the pub. No brewer's renovation had modernized the Feathers. It consisted of one room with a long bar. There was a pool table at one end. It was surprisingly full with rough-looking men.

'Feels like a villains' pub,' said Harry uneasily.

'It'll do,' said Agatha. She ordered a bottle of

beer for Harry and an orange juice for herself and they retreated to one of the few free tables.

'So what have you found out?' asked Agatha.

Harry told her about the necklace. 'I'd swear they were real diamonds,' he said. 'What if Wayne has the jewels from the robbery?'

'Keep your voice down,' ordered Agatha. All the tables were very close together. A thickset man was at the next table on their left. There was something about his stillness that made Agatha afraid he was listening.

'I think we should tell the police,' said Harry, lowering his voice.

'They'd never get a search warrant just because you thought a necklace was real diamonds. Besides, I'd like to show them that the detective agency can find out what they can't. Is there any hope you could take Wayne and Chelsea out this evening?'

'I'll try. What do you plan to do?'

'Wait till they leave the hotel and search their room.'

'How? The door will be locked.'

'Let me think. I know. If you can't get them to go out with you, we'll watch and see if they leave. If they do, you chat up that ditzy receptionist and I'll pinch their key.'

'Lot of ifs in your plans.'

'We've got to try. Can you really tell genuine diamonds from fake?'

'The sun shone on that necklace and it sparkled the way only real diamonds can sparkle.'

'Okay, but there are very good fakes. Still, we've got nothing else. Don't bother to ask them out. I'd feel better if you were with me when I get a look at their room.'

When they returned separately to the hotel, the receptionist handed Agatha a postcard sent by special delivery showing a view of Dover Castle. It was from James. 'Come and join me,' she read. 'I will be with friends outside Marseilles.' Name and address followed.

Agatha's lips tightened. He had simply driven off in a huff and now he expected her to make her own way to the south of France. She ignored the inner Agatha, who was longing to go.

Before she had parted from Harry, she had arranged that she should lurk in reception that evening to see if Wayne and his wife went out. If they did, she would phone Harry in his room so that he could come down and distract the receptionist.

There was little else she could do that dismal day, and the hours dragged on leaving her nothing else to think of but James.

By early evening, she was seated in a corner of the reception area, hidden behind a magazine. Did Wayne find the food at the hotel as awful as she did? The evening meal was not included, so there was no incentive for him to dine in the hotel.

At eight o'clock, to her relief, she peered over

her magazine in time to see Wayne and Chelsea make their way out of the hotel. She took out her mobile phone, dialled the hotel and was put through to Harry's room. 'They've gone,' she whispered. 'Be right down,' replied Harry.

Agatha waited anxiously until she heard him running lightly down the stairs. There was a creaky old lift, which juddered and shuddered up through the floors of the old hotel and hardly ever seemed to be available, so people used the stairs.

She waited to hear Harry chat up the receptionist, but he went straight to the hotel door and looked out. Then he shouted to the receptionist, 'You'll never believe it. Come and see this!'

'What?'

She left the desk and went to join him. Agatha darted to the desk, went behind it and lifted down the key to Wayne's room. Harry had found out the number earlier. She scurried back to her seat and raised her magazine just as Harry and the receptionist came back. 'I don't know where he went to,' Harry was saying. 'But it was this man on stilts walking past with a monkey on his shoulder. There must be a circus in town.'

'Haven't heard of it.' The receptionist, Betty Teller, went behind the desk again. Harry made for the stairs, and after a few moments Agatha followed him.

She caught up with him on the first landing. 'I've got the key,' she said triumphantly. They walked up to the next floor and along a corridor.

'Here we are,' Harry was just saying when they heard the creaking and groaning of the lift.

They retreated to the end of the corridor and round a corner. With a sinking heart, Agatha heard Wayne's voice. 'I'm telling you, I left my key at the desk not long ago.' The receptionist could then be heard protesting, 'Well, it's not there. I'll let you in with the pass key.'

They heard the sound of the lift clanking to a halt, the clatter of the old-fashioned gate being drawn back and, shortly after that, the sound of a key being turned in the lock.

'I'll go downstairs right now and look for it again, Mr Weldon,' said the receptionist.

'That's that,' muttered Agatha. 'We may as well try again tomorrow. Can you somehow get down there and throw the key on the floor or something?'

'Will do. What are you going to do now?'

'Get myself something to eat, I suppose.'

Sitting alone at a table in the Chinese restaurant, Agatha pulled the postcard from James out of her handbag. She had a weak longing to go and join him.

After she had finished her meal, she took out her phone and dialled Mrs Bloxby's number. Agatha had no intention of telling Mrs Bloxby about James's desertion, but no sooner had she heard her friend's sympathetic voice on the line than she blurted it out. 'He even sent me a

72

postcard with an address outside Marseilles asking me to join him,' she said.

'You are not going to, are you?'

'No,' said Agatha, fighting back a desire to cry.

'What has been going on? I read a bit about it in the newspapers.'

Agatha told her as much as she knew and described the abortive attempt to find the jewellery.

'Could you speak up?' pleaded Mrs Bloxby. 'The line's bad.'

Agatha looked around. There was no one near her. The only other customers were a middle-aged couple and a man in workman's overalls, so she raised her voice. When she had finished, Mrs Bloxby said seriously, 'Do be careful. It all sounds very dangerous.'

She began to chat about village gossip and Agatha felt soothed when she had rung off. It was only then that Mrs Bloxby realized she had failed to tell Agatha that Sir Charles had been looking for her.

Betty Teller, the receptionist, took a last look around on the floor behind the desk and let out an exclamation when she saw the key. She wondered whether to phone young Mr Weldon and then decided to tell her replacement, who was due on duty any minute, to do it.

Her replacement, a sour-looking Croatian named Nick Loncar, was late as usual. When he finally arrived she was so angry with him that she forgot to tell him about the key. Nick waited until she had gone and then nipped through to the bar and ordered a double whisky. He had just downed it when he heard the bell ring at the desk.

It turned out to be the last of the guests, other than Agatha and her party, checking out. They were an elderly couple. He listened with an impassive face to the all-too-familiar complaints of how the hotel had gone downhill and how awful the food was.

He ordered them a taxi and carried their bags to the door. He held out his hand for a tip, but they ignored him. Swearing under his breath, he returned to the desk.

By seven in the morning when the girl for the early shift, Kylie Smith, arrived, he was fast asleep. She nudged him awake. 'I got a call from Betty last night,' she said. 'She forgot to tell you that young Mr Weldon's room key was missing last night and she had to let him in with the pass key. She found his key later on the floor behind the desk. She says you'd better phone him and tell him.'

'Stupid cow,' said Nick, whose command of the English language had improved in leaps and bounds since he had arrived in Britain eight months ago. 'But he won't be awake. You do it.'

He yawned and stretched and made his way out of the hotel.

Kylie waited until nine o'clock and phoned

Wayne's room. There was no reply. She phoned again at ten. Still no reply.

She left the desk and went up to his room. A DO NOT DISTURB sign was hanging outside the door. I'd better wake him, thought Kylie. The maid's got to get in to clean up. She knocked loudly on the door and called out, 'Mr Weldon!'

Cyril Hammond came along the corridor at that moment and asked her what was up. She explained about the key.

'Well, just use it and we'll go in and wake him up,' said Cyril. 'He and Chelsea probably got pissed last night and they're sleeping it off.'

Kylie unlocked the door and walked in. Then she screamed and screamed.

Chapter Five

Agatha was in her room telling Patrick about the failed attempt to find out whether Wayne had the jewels, when they heard screams. They both ran out into the corridor. Agatha's room was on the third floor. The screams were coming from the floor below. They both ran down.

Cyril Hammond was holding Kylie in his arms and trying to calm her down. 'I'll need to call the police,' he was saying.

'What's up?' asked Agatha.

Cyril nodded in the direction of Wayne's room. Agatha and Patrick looked in. Wayne was lying on his back, his T-shirt covered in blood. Chelsea was lying over by the window, the side of her head blown away. A few feathers from a pillow lying on the floor drifted in a draught from the window.

'Shot through the pillow,' muttered Patrick. 'Tried to deaden the sound.'

Kylie's screams still rent the air. Agatha went back to her and slapped her soundly across the face and she dissolved in sobs.

Agatha took out her phone and called the police. Then she turned to Cyril. 'You'd best take this girl downstairs and get her some sweet tea or something to calm her down.'

Patrick waited until they had gone. Then he extracted the key from the lock and wiped it thoroughly with a handkerchief, and holding it by the handkerchief, put it back in the lock again.

'You're destroying evidence,' gasped Agatha.

'Exactly. No doubt the murderer wore gloves. I'll bet neither you nor Harry did when you were handling the key. We'll all be fingerprinted.'

Guilty thoughts raced through Agatha's shocked brain. She had talked to Harry about the jewels in that pub. She had talked again to Mrs Bloxby about them. What if Charlie Black, the armed robber, had been one of the listeners?

The police arrived, headed by Detective Inspector Barret. He told Agatha and Patrick to wait downstairs.

Harry was already there, having heard the grim news from one of the maids.

'They're going to find out about that missing key,' said Agatha.

'They'll assume the murderer took it,' said Patrick. 'I mean, he must have. You say Harry left it on the floor behind the desk. The girl probably found it and put it back. We're all in for a lot of hard questioning. I think Harry here should tell them about that necklace. The sooner they start looking for Charlie Black, the better.'

'And how are all the happy holidaymakers?' asked a cheerful voice behind them.

They swung round. Charles Fraith stood there, the smile dying on his face as he saw their strained looks.

'What's happened?' he asked.

James Lacey finally reached the villa owned by his friends, Kenneth and Mary Clarke. Before his retirement from the army, he had done a short desk stint at the Ministry of Defence. That was where he had got to know Kenneth along with the Hewitts, now retired to Ancombe. He had kept in touch with Kenneth, learning that Kenneth on his retirement had decided to set up a bed and breakfast in France. He remembered Kenneth as a round, jolly man with a charming wife.

But the Kenneth who came out to welcome him had changed. He looked so much older and had lost weight. His once thick grey hair was now thin and his pink scalp shone though. He was wearing a Hawaiian beach shirt and droopy grey cotton shorts and open leather sandals with black socks.

'Come in,' he cried. 'Mary's down at the shops. She'll be back soon. You're our only guest, so we'll have plenty of time to catch up on the gossip.'

'Is she here?' asked James.

'Who?'

'My ex. Agatha Raisin.'

'No, old chap. Were you expecting her?'

'I sent her your address. I expected her to join me.'

'Might come along later. Let's have a drink. I'll show you to your room first.'

The bedroom had a double bed, a large Provençal wardrobe, one easy chair and a washbasin with a mirror above over by the window.

'Just leave your things,' said Kenneth. 'We'll sit in the garden.'

He led the way back downstairs and through a cluttered messy kitchen and out into the back garden, where chairs and tables had been placed on a stone terrace overlooking a weedy and uncultivated garden.

'So how are things?' asked James, accepting a glass of the local wine and wondering where Agatha was. Surely she would come and join him. He thought ruefully of the times he had changed his holiday destination just to make sure that Agatha did *not* join him.

'To tell you the truth, I'm a bit homesick. Gets lonely up here when we don't have guests.'

'What about the locals?'

'Difficult to get to know. Never could master the language.'

'Can't you learn? Surely it would help.'

'Fact is,' said Kenneth moodily, 'I'm homesick. I'd swap all this for rainy London. Damned euro. Everything's so expensive.'

'You've got a big garden. You could grow your own vegetables.'

'My back hurts,' said Kenneth.

They heard the sound of a car. 'That'll be Mary. She's dying for some company.'

They heard the front door open. Kenneth shouted, 'In the garden, darling. James is here.'

James remembered Mary as a neat blonde woman. As she came on to the terrace, he barely recognized her. Her hair was grey and she had put on weight. She was wearing a faded blue housedress and her bare feet were thrust into a pair of battered espadrilles.

'How are you, James?' She gave him a peck on the cheek. 'Do pour me a glass of wine, darling. It was hot as hell in the town. So what have you been up to, James, since we last saw you?'

'I wrote a military history, but now I'm writing travel books.'

'How splendid! Give us a plug. We could do with the business.'

'What about August? All the Parisians flock south.'

'Well, they aren't flocking here.'

'Have you advertised?'

'Oh, yes,' sighed Kenneth. 'Put a small ad in the *Spectator*.'

'What about the French newspapers?'

'We never actually thought of having French people here,' said Mary. 'We advertised good English home cooking.'

'Maybe not a good idea,' said James. 'The

English like to come to France for French cooking and the French won't like the idea of English cooking either.'

'Oh, what do you know about it?' Mary's voice had a waspish tone. 'You're a bachelor. No cares. You're not stuck in this stinking hot villa miles from anywhere. It was Kenneth's idea. I sometimes think men never grow up. When we had our first guests, all he wanted to do was play host while I slaved in the kitchen.'

There was an awkward silence. I want to get out of here, thought James. But I'd better suffer it for a day or two in case Agatha does turn up. Aloud he said, 'Why don't I take the pair of you for lunch in Marseilles?'

They both brightened. 'That would be great,' said Kenneth.

So James entertained them at an outdoor restaurant on the Corniche where Mary ate too much and Kenneth drank too much. The hard sun glittered on the water.

And then James saw a stocky woman with good legs walking towards the restaurant. She was wearing a large straw hat and dark glasses. Agatha at last.

He leaped to his feet. 'Agatha! Over here!'

The woman removed her sunglasses and stared at him blankly. James actually blushed and sat down hurriedly. 'Sorry,' he called to her. 'A mistake.'

*　　*　　*

Charles leaned back in his chair and surveyed the group. 'You're in for some hard questioning from the police. They'll want to know why you didn't tell them about your suspicions.'

'I'm not going to tell them.' Agatha looked strained and weary. 'What would they have done anyway if Harry had told them about that necklace? Nothing, that's what. It wouldn't have been enough to justify a search warrant.'

Her heart sank as Betty Teller walked into the hotel. A policeman led her towards a little-used smoking room which the police had commandeered as an office. They would take Betty through the events of yesterday evening. They would ask her if she had left the desk. She might tell them about Harry calling her to the door.

'I'd better check in,' said Charles, getting to his feet. 'Where's James?'

'He decided to visit friends in the south of France.'

'Typical,' said Charles cheerfully.

Agatha watched his well-tailored figure approach the desk, now manned by the manager, Mr Beeston. Agatha never knew whether Charles was fond of her or simply looked on her as someone who occasionally provided interesting diversions.

After ten minutes, Betty Teller emerged. 'Mrs Raisin,' called the policeman. Agatha suppressed a groan and walked into the smoking room.

'Mrs Raisin,' began Barret, 'first of all, I would like to know why you are still here and why two members of your staff are here also. We checked up on you. That unsavoury-looking youth, Harry Beam, is employed by you, as is Patrick Mulligan. You all had your photographs in the newspaper a year ago. Mr Lacey, your companion, has left.'

'It was my scarf that was used in the first murder,' said Agatha defensively. 'I am a detective. I felt compelled to stay on to see if we could find out who had committed the murder.'

'Indeed. Now to yesterday evening. Betty Teller, the receptionist, said that you were sitting in reception, reading a magazine, when Harry Beam came down the stairs. He walked to the door and called to her. He told her he had just seen a man on stilts with a monkey on his shoulder, but she could not see anyone there. Did you take the key to Wayne Weldon's room?'

'No.'

'This is only the initial interview. You will be asked to report at the station later, make a full statement, and sign it. Why do you think Harry Beam lied?'

'I really don't know.' Agatha felt herself becoming flushed and cross. 'Maybe he didn't lie. Maybe he fancied the receptionist.'

'We'll ask him. Now, why do you think Mr Weldon and his wife were murdered? Do you think they knew the killer of Mrs Jankers?'

Agatha decided to tell the truth. 'I found out that Mrs Jankers's second husband, Charlie Black, robbed a jewellery store, but the jewellery was never been recovered. Harry noticed that Chelsea Weldon was wearing a necklace that looked like real diamonds. I think they may have had the jewellery and Charlie Black may have murdered both of them for it.'

'These suspicions of yours – did you tell anyone else, apart from your colleagues?'

'No, certainly not.' Agatha felt uneasy, thinking of how she had talked about the jewels in that pub and then in the restaurant.

'I think you stole the key to that room,' said Barret. 'I think you waited until young Weldon and his wife went out and went upstairs.'

'Of course not,' said Agatha, glad now that Patrick had had the foresight to wipe that key clean.

'Right, just you wait there. We'll get Mr Beam in here and see if your stories match.'

Harry was summoned. He must have made a lightning change of clothes, thought Agatha. The studs had been removed. He was wearing a plain charcoal-grey suit, striped shirt and silk tie.

'Sit down on that chair next to Mrs Raisin,' ordered Barret. 'Now, yesterday evening, why did you distract the receptionist by telling her that fairy story about a man on stilts?'

'I was considering chatting her up,' said Harry. 'I felt like having some young company for a change.'

Agatha winced.

'Then I spotted Mrs Raisin in reception. I hadn't noticed her before because she had been

84

hidden behind the magazine she was reading. Mrs Raisin expects us to work all hours of the day. So I dropped the idea.'

Barret studied him for a long moment. Then he said, 'I want both of you to stay in the hotel. A policeman will call for you later and take you both down to the station, where you will make official statements.'

At that moment, the door opened and the policeman who had been on guard outside said, 'A word with you, sir. It's urgent.'

Barret joined him. They went out together. Agatha half rose to leave. 'Sit down!' barked Detective Sergeant Wilkins.

The door opened again and Barret called, 'Wilkins!'

The detective went out to join him. A policewoman was seated in a corner of the room. Had she not been there, Agatha would have pressed her ear to the door.

At last Barret came back, looking excited. 'You two can go,' he said. 'We'll be in touch later.'

'What's happened?' asked Agatha.

'Mind your own business.'

Charles Fraith had been joined by Cyril and his wife. 'This is awful,' said Cyril. 'Why are the police going away? We were told to wait to be interviewed.'

'Something's happened,' said Agatha, 'that's sent them running off.' Dawn Hammond was crying quietly.

'Where's Patrick?' Agatha asked Charles.

'He went up to his room to make some calls.'

'I think we should go up and join him. He may have heard something.'

'Give me his room number,' said Charles. 'I'll join you there. I haven't unpacked yet.'

James sat gloomily nursing a glass of wine in the villa garden. Perhaps it was just as well that Agatha hadn't joined him. Kenneth moaned constantly about the folly of having ever left Britain and of having sunk his savings into this bed and breakfast.

Mary drank quite a lot and complained so much about the price of food that at last James suggested he pay for his visit just as if he were a customer. He had expected his generous offer to be refused and was quite taken aback when it was accepted with alacrity.

Mary came out into the garden and placed a radio on the table. 'Just going to get the news on the BBC World Service,' she said. 'It's like a little bit of home.'

For heaven's sake, thought James impatiently, you would think she was in Outer Mongolia.

She switched on the radio in time for the Greenwich time signal, followed by the strains of 'Lilliburlero'. The news began. A bomb explosion in a busy street in Toronto, an outbreak of cholera in Bangladesh, protesters in Africa demonstrating over the cull of elephants, and the discovery of a mummy in Egypt.

'They hardly ever give any news of home,' complained Mary. 'You would think there still was a British Empire the way they go on.'

'Shh!' admonished James, for the announcer had gone on to say, 'There was a shooting yesterday evening in the quiet seaside town of Snoth-on-Sea. Wayne Weldon, son of the Geraldine Jankers who was recently found strangled to death on the beach, was found shot in his hotel room along with his wife, Chelsea. Now, to our main story. A bomb went off in the early hours of this morning in a busy street in Toronto . . .'

'Excuse me. I've got to use the phone,' said James, getting to his feet.

'Just put the money for the call next to the box on the table in the hall,' said Mary.

'I'll use my mobile.'

James went up to his room and dialled the Palace Hotel and asked to be put through to Agatha's room. He waited impatiently. At last he was told there was no reply. 'Can you page her?' he asked. There was another long silence, and then the manager came on the line. 'Mrs Raisin's friend, Sir Charles Fraith, has arrived,' said Mr Beeston, proud of having a title staying at his hotel. 'I'll try his room, if you like, sir. Mrs Raisin may be there.'

'Don't bother,' said James.

He rang off and sat staring out of the window. In the hope that Agatha might arrive after all, he had booked for two weeks and paid in advance.

Now she had Charles with her, he thought bitterly, she would not bother to come. He wanted to leave. He knew he wouldn't get a refund, but the thought of enduring another day of Kenneth and Mary was too much for him. He would go back to Carsely and immerse himself in work. He had a travel book on Tunisia to write. He had travelled extensively in that country and had all his notes. It was odd, but he had always assumed Agatha would follow him wherever he went. For the first time he realized how much Agatha's unstinting adoration meant to him. The only thing that made him glad she had not come was the knowledge that she would have hated it as much as he did.

Agatha, Harry, Patrick and Charles were seated in Patrick's room. 'I wonder what's up,' said Agatha.

'I can't go along to the police station,' said Patrick. 'There's a policeman on guard outside the hotel.'

'Is there anyone you could phone?'

'I've got a contact at the station, but he won't want to speak to me if there's something important going on.'

There was a tentative tap at the door. 'Come in,' shouted Agatha.

Cyril and his wife Dawn entered. 'This is terrible,' said Cyril. 'Poor Wayne. Poor Chelsea. Who could have done such a thing?'

'It could be that ex-husband of Mrs Jankers,' said Patrick. 'He's just out of prison and he might have come looking for the jewels.'

'Wayne wouldn't have had them,' exclaimed Cyril. 'I mean, after all this time. Charlie got twelve years.'

He focused his attention on Harry. 'What's he doing here?'

'Harry works for me. And this is Sir Charles Fraith, a friend of mine.'

'I'm frightened,' wailed Dawn. 'What if we're next?'

'Well, I'm hungry,' said Charles. 'We could all go to the dining room.'

'Not there.' Agatha repressed a shudder. 'The food's awful.'

Harry picked up a copy of the Yellow Pages. 'I'll order something in. What about pizza?'

'That'll do,' said Charles. 'I'll take your drink orders and we'll get them up from the bar.'

Harry searched the Yellow Pages. 'Got it,' he said. 'Luigi's Pizzeria. What about just getting simple ones like cheese and tomato?'

They all agreed. Harry phoned and gave the order and told them to deliver the pizzas to the hotel room.

'How is Mr Jankers?' asked Patrick.

'He's lying down. He says he's not ill but it's all been a great shock,' said Cyril.

They talked in a desultory manner until the drinks and then the pizzas arrived.

'I wish I could get out and see what's happening,' said Harry. 'There must be a fire escape here.'

'There's a fire escape at the end of the corridor,' said Agatha. 'You could try that way, but don't get caught.'

Harry quickly finished his pizza. 'I'll see if I can discover anything.'

Harry went along the corridor and pushed open the fire door. He wedged a business card in it to keep it open and then went nimbly down the rusty stairs.

He found himself in an unkempt garden. He saw a gate leading on to the promenade. It was padlocked and chained. He climbed over it. Waves were buffeting the sea-front and washing across the promenade.

He ran along the front, keeping to the buildings, pausing as a particularly large wave smashed over, and then running on when it retreated. There were sandbags outside some of the houses to stop them from being flooded.

Harry wondered why the council didn't do anything about the increasingly high tides.

He turned off towards the police station and saw a crowd of reporters and photographers outside.

'What's going on?' he asked one reporter.

'We just know the police brought a man in for questioning. He had a blanket over his head, so we couldn't see him. The police say they'll make a statement later.'

Harry couldn't find out any more, so he dodged the waves again and got back to the hotel.

When he reached Patrick's room, there was a note in the door. 'Downstairs in the bar.'

Harry went down and found the party minus Cyril and his wife. 'Where's Cyril gone?' he asked.

'Upstairs, comforting Mr Jankers.'

The day dragged on and it was six o'clock before Detective Inspector Barret and Detective Sergeant Wilkins arrived.

Cyril and Dawn joined them in the bar, having been summoned by the detectives.

'We have arrested Charles Black, Mrs Jankers's ex-husband,' said Barret. 'He was spotted in a pub outside the town called the Feathers.' Agatha winced. Charlie had probably been in the bar when she and Harry had been discussing the jewels. 'We found a quantity of jewellery in his car along with a sawn-off shotgun. It's an open-and-shut case. He has been charged with the murders of Wayne and Chelsea Weldon.'

Cyril brightened. 'That means we're free to leave.'

'I'm afraid not,' said Barret. 'You, Mrs Raisin, and your travelling circus may leave, but I am afraid that you, Mr Hammond, your wife and Mr Jankers will need to stay a few days longer.'

'Why?' wailed Dawn.

'It appears that on the night Mrs Jankers was

murdered, Charles Black was in London at a gambling club and did not leave until two in the morning. There are plenty of witnesses to attest to that fact. So that leaves us with the unsolved murder of Geraldine Jankers. We will be back tomorrow to take both of you and Mr Jankers over your earlier statements.'

'We'll never get out of here,' moaned Dawn.

'So what are we going to do now?' asked Patrick after the Hammonds and the detectives had left.

'Wait!' Agatha took out her phone and called Phil Marshall. 'How are things going at the agency?' she asked.

'I wish you'd get back here,' said Phil. 'There's a lot of work come in and I can barely cope.'

'I'll see what I can do.' Agatha rang off.

'There's a lot of work back in Mircester. I think you, Patrick, and you, Harry, should return to the office. If I get any leads, I'll let you know.'

'Alone at last, darling,' said Charles the next morning after they had waved goodbye to Patrick and Harry.

'I hope you are here to help me,' said Agatha. 'The trouble is if you see some pretty girl you know, you'll be off like a shot.'

'I don't know anybody in the whole wide world who would want to visit a place like this. I haven't seen the mysterious Mr Jankers.'

'I suppose I'd better start all over again,' sighed Agatha, 'in case Mr Jankers might have some idea. Cyril had known Geraldine for a long time. Maybe she knew something unsavoury about him and threatened to tell his wife. Let's go up to Fred Jankers's room.'

Fred Jankers was sitting in a chair wrapped in a blanket. 'It's the shock of all this,' he said. 'I can't seem to get warm.'

Agatha introduced Charles and then asked, 'Did the police inform you that Charles Black has been arrested for the murders of Wayne and Chelsea?'

'Yes. I want to go home, but they say I've to stay here for a bit because they are still invest-igating Geraldine's death.'

'In the short time you knew your wife, did she seem afraid of anyone?'

He shook his head. 'Geraldine wasn't afraid of anyone.'

'Not even of Charlie Black?'

'No. Not as far as I know.'

'When you first met her at ballroom dancing, was there anyone else in the offing? I mean, did she seem romantically involved with anyone?'

He wrinkled his brow and pulled the blanket closer up to his chin. 'Let me think. She did come along with some chap. What was his name? Peter somebody.'

'Where was this dancing class?'

'In Lewisham.' He lowered the blanket and fished his wallet out of his pocket. 'I think I still have their card.' He took a small pile of cards out of his capacious wallet and flicked through them. 'Ah, here it is. "Jane and Jon's Ballroom Dancing, Cherry Street, Lewisham."'

Agatha took the card. 'I'll just borrow this for the time being.'

When they left Mr Jankers, Agatha said, 'We may as well go up to London tomorrow. I can't get much more out of Cyril or his wife or Fred Jankers. Who knows? She had a habit of annoying people. She was once married to a criminal. Blast! I wonder if Charlie did the job himself. Say he had an accomplice and the accomplice was after the jewels and got down here before Charlie. Let's see if this place has a library so we can check the old newspapers.'

When they went downstairs, Mr Beeston was checking in members of the press and looking delighted with this unexpected custom.

Agatha saw Cyril in the bar and went in, followed by Charles. 'That armed robbery,' she asked Cyril, 'when exactly did it take place?'

'Let me see – Charlie was on remand for six months before it got to court. It would be in 1994. In October, I think it was.'

They thanked him and went out in search of the library, finding it among the winding streets that formed part of the original town. It was a red sandstone building, or rather, it had been red, but it was one of those buildings that had never been cleaned up, and so it was mostly black with old soot.

They went in and found the newspaper section. Whatever money had been stinted on the outside of the building had been used on the inside, which was bright, cheerful and modernized. But they met with a setback. The library only contained records of what had been in the local papers. They went back out again and found a nearby pub.

Agatha took out her phone and called a journalist she used to know and asked if he could look up the records for an armed robbery that had taken place in October of '94 at a jeweller's in Lewisham, promising him an exclusive if she solved a murder case she was on. She gave him her mobile phone number and he said he would ring her back.

'So what really happened to dear James?' asked Charles.

'He cleared off. I told you.'

'Oh, really? I thought you two were off on a second honeymoon or something.'

'When the police told us we were free to leave this horrible burg, he suggested we go on holiday somewhere in the south of France. But I couldn't leave the case, so off he went. He sent me a postcard with the address, expecting me to join him, but I didn't feel like it.'

'Good heavens, Aggie grows up at last.'

'Don't call me Aggie!'

Agatha's phone rang. The journalist said, 'You

could have found it yourself on your computer. Here it is. Armed robbery. One Charles Black arrested. His partner got away.'

'Have you got a name for the partner?'

'Pete Silen. Police were looking for him but never found him.'

Agatha thanked him and hung up. 'He says Charlie's partner was a man called Pete Silen. The police never got him. Now our Geraldine turned up on the dance floor initially with someone called Peter.'

'Long shot.'

'But worth trying. We'll go tomorrow.'

Chapter Six

Agatha and Charles drove off early and headed for London. Agatha was glad that Charles was driving because she had slept badly and knew that the traffic on the way to Lewisham would be horrendous.

Agatha wondered how long Charles would stay on the case. In the past, he had had a habit of suddenly deciding to leave her, either because he had a date or because he had become bored. He led a self-contained, orderly bachelor life and maintained that lifestyle by doing exactly what he wanted, when he wanted to.

They stopped at a roadside restaurant for breakfast.

'Why should James want to take me to such a dreadful place?' Agatha burst out. 'He said he used to go there as a child.'

'He's in his fifties, isn't he?' asked Charles. Agatha nodded. 'So we're talking about a little over forty years ago. Probably was a sweet little watering hole then. Shops selling ice cream and postcards, Punch and Judy and donkey rides on the beach, things like that. I'll bet you he remembered every day as sunny as well. One does, and forgets all the rainy days. I mean, where did you go on holiday when you were a child?'

Agatha remembered occasional holidays at holiday camps with a shudder. Her parents were usually drunk and raucous.

'Here and there,' she said vaguely. 'Anyway, he's probably lazing in the south of France and basking in the sun. If you've finished your breakfast, we'd better get going.'

They circled around Lewisham until they found a car park. Charles looked up Cherry Street in the *London A to Z* he kept in the car. 'It's right off the High Street,' he said. 'Not far to walk. I see you've taken to wearing flat shoes. Ah, when love dies, women lose two and a half inches in height.'

'I'm not even going to reply to that,' said Agatha. 'Come on.'

Jane and Jon's Ballroom Dancing was situated above an antique shop. As they mounted the stairs, they could hear the strains of 'La Paloma'. 'Tango time,' commented Charles. 'I can just see you with a rose in your teeth, Aggie.'

'Stop being frivolous,' snapped Agatha. 'This is a murder investigation, remember?'

They opened the door and went in. Six couples were gyrating in a genteel version of the tango. A tall thin woman wearing a leotard and black tights came forward to meet them.

'Are you interested in joining the class?' she asked. She thrust out a bony hand. 'I'm Jane.'

'I'm a private detective,' said Agatha, 'and this is Sir Charles Fraith.'

Jane looked alarmed. Her pencilled eyebrows rose nearly into her black hair. 'It's all rubbish,' she said. 'I never touched the silly man.'

'I don't know what you're talking about.'

'Didn't Mrs Smither send you?'

'Never heard of her.'

Jane visibly relaxed. 'We've had some trouble because some woman is claiming I made a pass at her husband, but you should see Mr Smither! Fat and fifty, my dear.'

The music stopped. 'Excuse me,' said Jane. She started the CD over again and called, 'Once more and put some *feeling* into it.'

Agatha wondered why Jane was dressed more for a ballet class than for ballroom dancing. As if reading her thoughts, Jane said, 'I take them through some ballet exercises first to limber them up. Now what can I do for you?'

Agatha told her about the murder of Geraldine and how Geraldine had first come to the classes with a man named Peter.

'Oh, I remember her,' said Jane. 'Seemed a quiet woman but quite a nifty dancer. I believe she hit it off with Mr Jankers very quickly and then we never saw Peter Brody again.'

'Are you sure his name was Brody? Not Silen?'

'Definitely Brody.'

'Do you know where he lives?'

'Come into the office and I'll find his address.' She turned to the class. '*Swoop*, Hugh. Swoop and *dip*.'

The small man called Hugh dipped so far, his partner fell to the floor with him on top of her.

'Leave the swoop for the moment,' said Jane in a tired voice. And to Agatha, 'Follow me.'

'Is Jon your husband?' asked Agatha as Jane led them into the cubicle that served as an office.

'He was.'

'Where is he now?'

'Pentonville.'

'In prison? Why?'

'Dealing drugs. So I've got to manage the business on my own.' She squeezed in behind a desk and switched on a computer. 'Let me see. Brody. Ah, here we are. Fifty-two B Carriage Way.'

'Where is Carriage Way?' asked Charles.

'Go outside and turn right. It's the fourth turning on your right.'

They thanked her and left.

'I suppose we couldn't really expect this Peter to be Peter Silen,' said Agatha. 'I mean, if he was that easy to find, the police would have arrested him ages ago.'

'Still, he might shed some light on Geraldine's past,' said Charles. 'Here we are. Carriage Way. I thought with a name like that they'd be mews cottages.'

They walked along past tall stuccoed Victorian buildings until they came to number fifty-two. 'B must be the basement,' said Agatha.

They opened an iron gate and walked down

stone steps. 'No bell,' said Charles, knocking on the door.

A few moments passed and then the door was opened by a small wiry man wearing a tank top and stained jeans. He had sandy hair and small features: small brown eyes, small mouth and small nose. Charles guessed he was in his fifties.

'What do you want?' he asked.

Agatha launched into her spiel of being a private detective investigating the death of Geraldine Jankers.

'What's it to do with me?' he asked.

'Well, you used to escort Mrs Jankers to the ballroom classes. We thought if you could tell us a bit about her, about her friends, anyone who might have hated her, that sort of thing, it would be a great help.'

He hesitated for a moment and then said, 'Come in.'

He ushered them into a sparsely furnished but tidy living room. Apart from an old-fashioned hatstand loaded with coats, the furniture consisted of three hard upright chairs, a table and a large television set.

They sat down at the table. 'How did you meet Geraldine?' asked Agatha.

'I met her at the market. I was shopping, so was she. We got to talking and went for a drink. She said she had never learned to dance properly and one thing led to another and I volunteered to take her. I only went with her to two classes and then she got her claws into Jankers.'

'So you didn't know anything about her before then?'

'No. I thought it would be a bit of fun, but I tell you, I was fed up when she left me standing to go chasing after Jankers. Wait a moment. I thought the police got the murderer. Some armed robber.'

'Charlie Black murdered the son and his wife,' said Agatha. 'But he's got a cast-iron alibi for the night Mrs Jankers was killed.'

'Sorry, I can't help you. I thought she was nice at first but she turned out to be a bit of a bitch. I told her I was angry with her for getting me to sign on for the classes and then dumping me. She had seemed quite refined, but then she gave me a mouthful that would have made a sailor blush.'

'What do you do for a living, Mr Brody?' asked Charles.

'Oh, this and that. Why?'

'Just making conversation.'

Peter Brody seemed in that moment to change from quite an amiable man into someone hard and angry.

'Look, bugger off, the pair of you,' he said. 'I haven't got time for this. I'll show you out.'

Charles turned round as he and Agatha approached the door. 'Thank you for your time, Mr Silen,' said Charles.

Peter reached behind the hatstand and pulled out a sawn-off shotgun. He held it on them. 'Get back in the room.'

'It was a slip of the tongue,' said Charles desperately.

'Oh, yeah? Get in that room over there. Move it!'

They retreated before him. 'The police know where we are,' said Agatha.

'Move! Drop your handbag and leave it on the floor.'

He backed them into a room, empty except for a few packing cases, and then slammed the door on them and locked it.

Agatha and Charles looked at each other in dismay.

'Why did you call him Silen?' whispered Agatha.

'Because I felt he was lying. What are we going to do?'

Charles went to the window. It was barred. They could hear the sound of hurried movements coming from the other room.

'Have you got your phone?' asked Agatha.

'I left it behind,' mourned Charles.

They heard the outside door of the flat slam shut and then footsteps mounting the stairs.

'He's gone,' said Agatha. 'He may be back. We've got to get out of here. Can't you break the door down?'

Charles aimed a kick at the lock and then hopped around the room, moaning, 'I think I've broken my foot.'

'I'm going to look in these cases,' said Agatha. 'There might be something we can use. Stop howling and help me.'

But Charles sat on the floor nursing his foot. Agatha gave an exclamation of disgust and began to search in one of the packing cases. 'This one's full of car radios,' she said. She tried the next one. 'Leather jackets. No use. There must be something here we could use. Why couldn't he steal hardware?'

Charles fished in his pocket and held up a Swiss army knife. 'Look what I've got!'

'Oh, Charles, try and fiddle with the lock.'

'Should be able to do it. It's only a Yale.'

Charles extracted a thin blade from the knife and inserted it between the lock and the door jamb. The blade snapped in two. 'This can't be genuine,' he said.

'Where did you buy it?'

'At a market in Morocco. I'll try another blade.'

He inserted a stronger blade and tried again. Agatha waited in a fever of impatience. She was just beginning to say, 'Here, let me try,' when there was a snap and the door swung open.

'Right,' she said, seizing her handbag. 'Let's get out of here.'

'He's coming back,' cried Charles. 'Back in the room. He's probably got that gun with him.'

They darted back into the room and shut the door.

They heard Peter come in. Then they heard splashing sounds and the air was filled with the smell of petrol.

'He's going to burn us to death,' whispered Agatha. She took out her phone and called the police. 'Number fifty-two B Carriage Way,

104

Lewisham,' she said urgently. 'Armed man with shotgun about to burn the place down. For God's sake, hurry!'

The sinister splashing sounds continued outside.

'Give me one of those car radios,' whispered Charles.

'What for?'

'Just get it. We'll be burned to a crisp if we don't do anything.'

Agatha handed him a radio.

The door had not locked again. Charles eased it open. Peter was holding a can of petrol. His back was to Charles.

Charles raised the radio and brought it down with all his force on the back of Peter's head. Peter slumped unconscious to the floor.

'Come on, Aggie,' shouted Charles. 'Let's get out of here.'

They ran out and up the stairs and leaned against the railings, panting.

'Where the hell are the police?' raged Charles.

'At least we're safe.' Agatha opened her handbag and lit a cigarette.

'I wish you wouldn't do that. I hate smoking.'

'You smoke yourself – that is, when you can pinch someone else's cigarettes.'

'I don't any more. Haven't you heard about the dangers of passive smoking?'

'Bollocks. We're in the polluted open air of London.'

'You'll get wrinkles.' Charles seized the

cigarette from Agatha's fingers and threw it down the area steps.

'Don't ever do that again,' Agatha raged. Then there was a *whumph* and a sheet of flame roared up from the area steps just as the police and fire brigade arrived.

'There's a man in there,' shouted Charles.

'Stand back,' ordered a police inspector.

Agatha and Charles clutched each other as firemen shot water down into the basement.

'Now, who are you?' demanded the police inspector, 'And who's in there?'

More police had raced up the stairs to evacuate the flat above.

'In a moment,' said Agatha, watching anxiously as firemen with breathing apparatus began to descend the area steps.

She sighed with relief when a fireman slowly emerged with Peter slung over his shoulder.

Ambulance men rushed forward. Peter was put on a stretcher and an oxygen mask was placed over his face.

'Now,' said the police inspector.

Charles and Agatha eyed each other anxiously. Charles did not want to admit they had started the fire.

They gave their names and then began the long explanation of why they were there. 'I hit him with a car radio and knocked him out,' said Charles. 'That's how we made our escape. You see, it was when I called him Mr Silen that he panicked.'

'Why?'

'Because we believe he's Pete Silen, not Peter Brody. He was Charles Black's partner in the jewel theft – that is the Charles Black who has just been charged with murder.'

'So how did the fire start?' asked the inspector. 'I mean, it obviously started after you had knocked him out.'

Charles looked at Agatha. 'It was that man,' said Agatha. 'He was walking past smoking and he threw his cigarette down the area steps. Silen must have splashed some petrol outside as well as inside.'

'You'd best come down to the police station and make a full statement.'

Mrs Bloxby answered the door and found James Lacey on the steps.

'Mr Lacey. How nice. Do come in. How was your holiday?'

He followed her into the vicarage drawing room and sat down on the sofa with a sigh. 'Not very good, actually.'

Mrs Bloxby had no intention of telling him that she knew he had deserted Agatha.

'What happened?'

'We could have left Snoth-on-Sea . . .'

'Where?'

'Oh, it's a place I used to go to with my parents as a boy. I thought Agatha would love it, but it had all changed for the worse. Then there was this murder. When the police told us we were free to leave, Agatha refused to budge, so I went to the south of France to stay with friends who have a B and B there. I sent her a postcard, giving her the address and asking her to join me, but she didn't. I can't understand it.'

'Let me see,' said Mrs Bloxby gently. 'You left her in the middle of a murder inquiry and then expected her to make her own way to the south of France?'

'Put like that, it sounds bad. But she agreed to go on holiday with me. Maybe I should go back and give her a hand. She has a talent for running into danger.'

'I believe Sir Charles is still with her.'

I'm enjoying this, thought Mrs Bloxby. Oh dear.

James's face darkened. 'That's all right then. I had better go home and get on with my work.'

As he walked from the vicarage, he felt the pangs of emotional indigestion. James was not used to feeling guilty, particularly about anything to do with Agatha. He tried to tell himself that it was all her own fault, but finally came to the miserable conclusion that he had behaved like a selfish bastard. Agatha had spoilt him by being always adoring and always available. He had an uneasy feeling that he had lost her respect and affection for good.

It was evening by the time Charles and Agatha were released by the police. They were both tired and felt bludgeoned by all the questioning.

As they drove off, Agatha said, 'They made me

feel like a criminal. Why hadn't we shared our suspicions with the police? What would they have done? We were only looking for someone called Peter. I mean, who would have thought that it would be Pete Silen?'

'Don't play the innocent, Aggie. We hoped it might turn out to be Silen.'

'But we didn't really expect to find him!'

'I'm hungry. All we've had is a sandwich. Let's stop somewhere and eat.'

Agatha was too tired to want to waste time sitting in some restaurant, so they bought take-away burgers, fries and Cokes and had them in the car.

'Nothing like junk food when you're feeling miserable. Now, back to the hotel. I could sleep for hours.'

It was midnight when they reached the hotel. They were confronted by a policeman on duty. 'Mrs Raisin? Sir Charles Fraith? You are to report to the police station immediately.'

'It's the middle of the night,' wailed Agatha.

'Those are my orders.'

'Come on,' said Charles wearily. 'May as well get it over with.'

Detective Inspector Barret and Detective Sergeant Wilkins were waiting for them in an interview room. Barret looked angry.

'You had important information about this case that you did not report to the police. You should have told us about Pete Silen.'

'It was only a guess,' said Agatha. 'We were only checking up on one of Mrs Jankers's old dancing partners. How were we to know he'd turn out to be a villain?'

'In the future, I want you to report anything significant to us before you set out to investigate it. Do I make myself clear?'

'Yes, yes. Stop shouting at me. I'm tired and I was nearly killed.' To Agatha's horror a tear slid down her cheek.

'Leave her alone,' said Charles angrily. 'All this could have waited until the morning.'

'Very well,' said Barret. 'I'll let you go. But remember, your amateur efforts are impeding a police investigation.'

'How?' yelled Agatha. 'If it hadn't been for us, the police would never have got Pete Silen.'

'Come on, Aggie,' said Charles. 'Let's get out of here.'

When Agatha finally said goodnight to Charles and was undressing, the phone rang. 'Now what?' she muttered, picking up the receiver.

It was Harry Beam. 'I've been trying you all evening,' he said. 'It was on television about Pete Silen.'

'Couldn't this call have waited until the morning?'

'It was just this. Did you know that Fred Jankers and his late missus lived in Lewisham? In fact, I think Fred still has a house there.'

'So?'

'It's quiet at the agency. Why don't I go to Lewisham and make some inquiries. Maybe the neighbours know a bit about the late Geraldine. There might be some other man in the picture. Do the police think Pete killed Geraldine?'

'I gather he has an alibi. All right, Harry. Go to Lewisham but keep in touch.'

Agatha rang off and got out of the rest of her clothes. She cleaned off her make-up but was too tired to take a shower. She crawled into bed and lay there shivering.

She could hear the sound of the waves pounding against the promenade outside.

There was a knock at the door and she let out a whimper of terror. 'Who's there?' she called.

'It's me. Charles.'

Agatha crawled out of bed and unlocked the door. 'I brought some brandy,' said Charles. 'Funnily enough, I can't sleep. Thought you might need a nightcap.'

'I could do with something,' said Agatha. 'I think I'm suffering from delayed shock. Aren't we supposed to be drinking hot sweet tea?'

'Probably. But brandy is cheerier.'

Charles found two tooth mugs in the bathroom and poured generous measures of brandy. He was wrapped in a brightly coloured dressing gown. Agatha had got back into bed. He handed her a glass of brandy and then sat on the bed beside her.

'Cheers, Aggie.'

'Cheers,' echoed Agatha.

After two glasses of brandy she began to feel warm and sleepy. She placed the empty glass on the bedside table, leaned back against the pillows, closed her eyes and fell instantly asleep.

Charles did not feel like going back to his own room. He got under the blankets next to her in the double bed and was soon asleep as well.

The ringing of the telephone on the bedside table next to him woke him in the morning. Charles picked it up. 'Hello?'

'This is James Lacey. I want to speak to Agatha. Is that you, Charles? What are you doing in her room?'

'What do you think?' said Charles cheerfully.

The phone at the other end was slammed down.

'Who was that?' asked Agatha sleepily.

'Some idiot wanting to know if we want breakfast. Go back to sleep. It's only seven in the morning.'

Harry Beam arrived in Lewisham the following morning armed with Fred Jankers's address, which had appeared in several of the newspapers after the murder of his wife.

The address was on the outskirts of Lewisham in a builder's development called Rosedown, where all the two-storeyed houses were identical and had a raw, recently built look. Harry had hoped to break in, but the gardens had no concealing trees or bushes. He was driving his white van.

He had with him a series of lock picks, but he knew it would take some time to open one of the doors and did not want to be observed by any of the neighbours as he fumbled with the lock.

He also did not want to spend all day waiting for darkness. He drove off until he found a quiet stretch outside an industrial estate. He stopped and got a pair of workman's overalls out of the van and a toolbox.

Then he returned to the house, stopped the van, and walked confidently up to the house and round to the back door. To his relief, there was a high hedge screening the back garden. He pulled on a pair of thin latex gloves and got to work with the lock picks. After a quarter of an hour, he managed to get the door open.

He found himself in the kitchen. It was a mess; Geraldine Jankers had obviously not bothered to clean up before she and her husband left. Dirty dishes were piled in the sink and there were the remains of a breakfast on the table.

He moved quietly through to the living room. A low coffee table was covered with glasses and bottles. Newspapers and magazines were scattered about. A set of bookshelves did not hold any books but various photographs of Geraldine. He went across a small square hall and opened a door on the other side, which revealed a dining room that looked as if it had hardly been used. He shut the door on it and opened a door next to it.

This, he judged, had been Fred's study. Unlike the other rooms, it was neat and tidy. Here were shelves of well-read books and a desk by the window had neatly arranged papers on it. He debated whether to pull the curtains, but decided against it. No one was moving on the street outside. He sat down and began to go through the papers. There was nothing of interest on the top of the desk except bills due to be paid. He opened the drawers. In a deep left-hand drawer he found clearly marked files – tax, VAT, insurance, bank – and decided it would not be worth going through them. He opened the right-hand drawer and found a file marked 'Personal Correspondence' and lifted it out.

At first, the contents seemed disappointing. Fred belonged to a bowling club and there were letters inviting him to various functions connected with it. There was one from Wayne saying he was looking forward to the holiday at Snoth-on-Sea. Modern Harry was amazed that people still wrote letters instead of texting messages, but he had noticed that Fred did not appear to own a computer. There was one from a ballroom dancing class, querying Fred's non-attendance. Then he found a small square envelope and opened it up.

The message was written in block capitals and simply said, IF YOU MARRY GERALDINE IT

114

WILL BE THE WORSE FOR YOU. It was signed ARCHIE SWALE.

Harry whistled under his breath. Here was something at last. Archie Swale was the old geezer who lived in Brighton and who had been married to Geraldine. He carefully replaced the letter in the file and put everything back in the desk.

He then proceeded to search the rest of the house. In the main bedroom, he searched through the bedside tables without finding anything of significance. He ripped the duvet and sheets off the bed and lifted up the mattress.

Lying on the box spring and gleaming in the faint light coming through the window he saw two gold watches, a diamond brooch, a sapphire-and-diamond necklace and four gold chains. So Charlie Black didn't get all the jewellery, he thought. Did Fred know about this?

Harry carefully made the bed up again. He went quietly downstairs and let himself out. Fortunately for him, the lock clicked back into place.

He walked briskly to his van and drove off. Once he was well clear, he stopped the van and phoned Agatha on her mobile and told her what he had found.

'The police should know about that jewellery,' said Agatha, 'but we can't tell them. And what about old Archie Swale? He can't have kil' Geraldine. He's just not strong enough. M that letter was simply to warn Fred wha' letting himself in for by marrying Geraldine. Good work, Harry. Charles and I will pay Archie a visit.'

Agatha and Charles drove to Medlow Square in Brighton to confront Archie Swale. 'We'd better try to find out what he was doing on the night of the murder,' whispered Agatha.

But when she saw Archie again as he stood in the doorway – elderly and frail – her heart sank. He surely could never have had the strength to strangle someone like Geraldine.

She introduced Charles, stressing his title. 'Where's the other fellow?' asked Archie.

'I don't know,' said Agatha, privately relieved to note that for the first time in her life she really did not care where James was. 'We just wanted to ask you a few more questions.'

'Oh, all right,' said Archie reluctantly. 'You'd better come in.'

When they were seated, Agatha asked, 'Did the police ask you where you were the night Geraldine was murdered?'

'The police haven't been near me, I'm glad to say.'

Charles stood up and began to prowl about the room.

'As a matter of interest, where were you?' asked Agatha.

'Here, watching television.'

Agatha decided to lie. 'Mr Jankers said you

sent him a threatening letter telling him it would be the worse for him if he married Geraldine.'

'I was just giving him a friendly warning from one man to another.'

'But your letter sounded threatening.'

'Wasn't meant that way. Look, I've been pretty patient with you, but you aren't the police. Get out and don't come here again.'

Archie's face was red with anger.

'Don't you want to find out who murdered your ex-wife?' asked Agatha.

'The only reason I would want to know would be to shake him by the hand. Now, get the hell out of here!'

He loomed over her, suddenly seeming powerful in his rage.

Agatha rose shakily and edged round him. 'Come along, Charles,' she said.

Outside, Agatha rounded on Charles. 'You were a fat lot of help.'

'Don't get your knickers in a twist, sweetie. I was looking at photographs. Do you know old Archie used to be in the paratroopers? There was a regimental photo of him and his buddies in that dark corner by the fireplace. He must have been very tough at one time.'

They got in the car. 'Well, he isn't tough now,' said Agatha.

'Think about it,' said Charles. 'A dark night, a man in a rage, a man who's been taught to kill. Geraldine all unsuspecting. She turns her back on him. He seizes the scarf and twists it

117

tight. He's still got powerful hands. Didn't you notice?'

'I don't think it could be him,' said Agatha stubbornly. 'I mean, Charlie Black didn't need to do the murder himself. He could have sent one of his villainous friends. Told him to find out from her where the jewels were and get them. Geraldine refuses and the villain loses his rag and murders her.'

'My money's on Archie,' said Charles.

James Lacey was once more Carsely's most wanted single man. Before she left, Agatha had bragged to Miss Simms, secretary of the Carsely Ladies' Society, about her holiday with James. Miss Simms had told the other members, and so it was noticed that James had returned on his own.

A newcomer to the village, Deborah Fanshawe, was particularly interested. She was in her forties, recently divorced, rich and attractive. She was a tall, leggy woman with masses of brown curly hair and a great deal of energy. Deborah was the ladies' society's newest member and considered a great acquisition. She organized sales of work and outings for the aged. She seemed to be indefatigable. Only Mrs Bloxby found her somewhat wearisome. When Deborah appeared on her doorstep yet again one morning, the vicar's wife found it hard to hide her irritation.

'I am very busy, Mrs Fanshawe,' she said.

'Just wanted a word,' said Deborah cheerfully.

'Oh, come in, but you can't stay long.'

Deborah sprawled out on the sofa. She always wore very short skirts and Mrs Bloxby averted her eyes from those long legs and the skirt that was hitched up to show an edge of frilly knickers.

'It's about James Lacey,' said Deborah. 'I am most definitely interested.'

Mrs Bloxby turned her mild gaze on her and said nothing.

'How do you think I should go about getting him?'

'My dear Mrs Fanshawe. That is entirely up to you. I have no advice to give.'

'But you're a friend of this Agatha Raisin. Is he still keen on her?'

'I suggest you ask him. Now, if there is nothing further . . .'

Deborah pouted and got to her feet. 'Well, I'll get him. Just you see.'

The vicar came in when Deborah had left. 'Who was that?'

'Mrs Fanshawe.'

'Tremendous lady. Such a help in the parish.'

'I think she has too many hormones,' said Mrs Bloxby and walked off to the kitchen, leaving her husband staring after her.

Agatha and Charles returned to the hotel. Betty

Teller was once more at the reception desk. She handed Agatha her key and then said, 'Letter for you.'

Agatha took the envelope. It had only her name on the front. It must have been delivered by hand.

She ripped it open. Written in block capitals was the simple message: YOU'RE DEAD.

Chapter Seven

Charles looked over her shoulder. 'Could be some nutter.'

'I'm taking this to the police,' said Agatha.

'Do you mind going on your own? I'm tired.'

'Charles! Someone could be out there waiting to murder me!'

'Tell you what, Aggie. Go up to your room. If you go to the police station, by the time they've finished with you the tide will be up and you'll need to run the gauntlet of the waves. They'll send someone.'

'All right,' said Agatha reluctantly.

Once in her room, she saw the bottle of brandy Charles had brought the night before. She poured herself a stiff measure and then phoned the police station and asked to speak to Barret.

When he came on the line, she told him about the threatening letter. 'I'll send someone to collect it,' said Barret. 'We'll let forensics have a look at it. It's your own fault. You should go back to Shitface-on-the-Wold, or wherever it is you come from.'

'I run a successful detective agency in Mircester,' said Agatha crossly.

'Whatever. I'll have someone along there in the next half-hour.'

Agatha sat and sipped her brandy. Then she decided to go down to reception and wait for the policeman.

When he finally arrived, he was soaking wet. He took the letter from her and put it in an envelope.

'Now I have to go back out and dodge the waves,' he said crossly. 'Two people were swept out to sea last year. If the council don't do something about it soon, we'll have more drownings, not to mention the whole front falling into the sea.'

When he had left, Agatha realized she was hungry. She went to the desk and phoned Charles's room. There was no reply.

She could wait until the tide retreated and go out into the town for something to eat. Agatha decided to brave the dining room in the hope that the food would not be so awful as the last time.

The dining room was empty except for Fred Jankers. The press had gone.

He looked across the room and saw her. 'Please join me,' he said.

Agatha thought he looked much better. He had regained colour in his cheeks and some sparkle in his eyes.

'What's on the menu this evening?' asked Agatha, sitting down opposite him.

'I don't know. The chef has left now that there's so few of us to cook for. They've got some woman in from the town. We're supposed to take pot luck.'

A waitress appeared bearing two bowls of soup. Agatha tentatively tasted it and then her eyebrows rose in surprise. 'This is delicious,' she said. 'Ham-and-pea soup.'

It was hard to make conversation because of the din of the waves outside. The soup was followed by roast lamb, roast potatoes and peas.

Fred suggested they order wine, but Agatha refused, so he ordered a half-bottle for himself.

'I don't know which has upset me more,' said Fred, 'the murder of my wife or this business about the jewels. I really didn't know anything about them. Poor Geraldine was a dark horse. They're going to release her body for burial. I suppose I'll have to bury Wayne and Chelsea as well.'

'Won't Chelsea's parents be responsible for her funeral?'

'She was an orphan. She lived with an aunt, but the aunt told me she didn't want to know anything about it. Quite shocking. She said she always knew Chelsea would come to a bad end.'

'Why?'

'She didn't like Wayne and she hated poor Geraldine. Made quite a scene at the wedding, she did. Drunk, of course.'

'Who inherits now that Wayne is dead?'

'I really don't know. I haven't been in touch with the solicitors recently. The police say I can leave, but somehow I can't. I really want to know who murdered my wife.'

'Did she ever talk about Archie Swale, her ex?'

'No, she never did. Never talked about Charlie either. She would say, "The past is past." One of her favourite sayings.'

I'll bet it was, thought Agatha cynically.

Charles paced up and down his room, wondering what to do. When the phone had rung, he had not answered it, being sure it was Agatha. His manservant, Gustav, had rung him on his mobile and said that Guy and Cynthia Partington were coming on a visit. They were Charles's great friends. They lived outside Inverness and he had enjoyed their hospitality during the grouse season.

But it would mean leaving Agatha in the lurch. He was tempted simply to pack up and disappear, except that Agatha might think he had been kidnapped and call out the police.

The really cheap and caddish thing would be to wait until she had gone to sleep and leave a note at the desk downstairs for her. Charles decided at last that the caddish way was the easiest.

He hung the DO NOT DISTURB notice outside his door and began to pack. The phone rang twice and then Agatha knocked at his door and called out, 'Charles, are you there?'

Affecting a sleepy voice, he shouted, 'I'm awfully tired. Going to sleep.'

'See you in the morning,' called Agatha.

Charles sat down to write that note. He lied and said that Gustav had phoned him in the middle of the night and that he had had to leave immediately. He waited until one in the morning, and then, carrying his suitcase, took the creaky lift downstairs. He handed the note to the night receptionist, Nick Loncar.

'I'll just get your bill, sir,' called Nick to Charles's retreating back. Charles turned and reluctantly approached the desk. He handed over a credit card and waited impatiently while Nick made out a receipt.

Then he walked out of the hotel and round to the car park.

The next morning, Agatha tried phoning Charles's room. No reply. She decided to go down for breakfast, hoping that the splendid local woman was on duty in the kitchen.

She was relieved to see the dining room was empty. Conversation with Fred had died the previous evening over the apple crumble. He had looked suddenly tired and had said he did not want to wait for coffee.

Betty Teller came in and handed her an envelope. 'This was left for you,' she said.

Agatha opened it gingerly, expecting another threatening letter. To her amazement, it was from Charles. 'Dear Aggie,' Charles had written. 'Got phoned by Gustav in the middle of the night. My aunt is very ill. Didn't want to wake you. Have to dash. Will phone. Love, Charles.'

'I don't believe it,' muttered Agatha. 'His aunt's as strong as a horse.' She knew Charles's aunt lived with him and sometimes answered the phone. She took out her mobile and dialled Charles's number. His aunt answered. 'Agatha Raisin here,' said Agatha. 'I heard you were very ill and –'

'Absolute nonsense,' came the robust voice. 'Goodbye.'

Agatha felt bereft. Charles knew that someone had threatened her and yet he had decided to clear off.

She stared across the bleak expanse of the dining room and tried not to cry. Then she decided to take action. She phoned Patrick. 'Can the agency spare you?' she asked. 'I need some help down here.'

'I don't think a few days would hurt,' said Patrick. 'I'll drive down today.' Agatha told him all she had learned so far and then rang off.

A waitress served her breakfast – fluffy scrambled eggs and bacon and a pot of excellent coffee. Despite her misery, Agatha resolved to tell Mr Beeston, the manager, that if he paid the local woman a good salary he might entice customers back to his hotel.

After breakfast she decided to go out shopping. The hotel did not have a laundry service and she was tired of washing out her underwear in the handbasin in her room. Much easier to buy new stuff.

She walked to the promenade wall and looked

out to sea. The tide was out and grey choppy waves stretched to the horizon under a grey sky.

Agatha had a sudden longing to be back in Carsely with her cats. Although she knew Charles's friendship was often fickle, she felt abandoned. The new Agatha Raisin, she told herself firmly, must give up any emotional reliance on men. Bugger them all. Who needed them?

She turned up a side street that led to the main street. There was a sex shop with a colourful display of gadgets in the window. A group of schoolgirls were staring in the window and giggling.

Whatever happened to romance? thought Agatha. Or will these girls grow up more sensible than me, never expecting any knight on a white charger to come along?

She went into Marks and Spencer and bought herself six pairs of knickers and three brassieres.

Agatha was emerging from the shop with her purchases when she collided with a tall man. Her shopping bags fell to the ground. 'Here! Let me.' He stooped and gathered up her bags and handed them to her. 'Sorry about that. I wasn't looking where I was going.'

Agatha smiled up at him. He was well dressed in a tailored suit and dark overcoat. His face was thin and tanned and his hair properly barbered.

'I recognize you!' he exclaimed. 'You're that woman detective. I saw your photo in the local paper. You must have a fascinating life. I say, have you time for a coffee?'

'That would be nice,' said Agatha. 'You haven't introduced yourself.'

'I'm Terry Armstrong.'

They walked together along the street. 'What are you doing here?' asked Agatha.

'I'm a builder. My men are working on some new houses locally. Here's a café. It's not too bad.'

He opened the door and ushered her in.

It was an old-fashioned tea shop, perhaps a relic of the days when James Lacey was a boy. There were lace covers on the tables and a large central wooden stand with layers of gorgeous-looking cakes.

Agatha took stock of her new companion. His accent was London, or so she thought. In her youth, each district of London had its separate accent, but now there was just one, if you excluded the Cockneys.

'Have you been on holiday?' she asked. 'That tan never came out of a bottle.'

'I've got a place in Marbella.'

'Building trade must be good.'

'I do pretty well.'

A waitress came up. He ordered a pot of coffee. Agatha refused an offer of cake.

'So tell me about your job,' he asked.

'If you've read the newspapers, I'm afraid you'll know as much as I do,' said Agatha. 'The police have arrested Charlie Black, the man who robbed the jeweller's, and now they've got Pete Silen, his partner, as well.'

'I read about Pete Silen. He nearly killed you.'

Agatha happily launched into a highly exaggerated account of her adventures in Lewisham.

When she had finished, he asked, 'And what about this friend of yours who was with you? Is he back at the hotel?'

Agatha's face darkened. 'He cleared off sometime during the night.' She shrugged. 'I'm afraid he's like that.'

'It's bit boring down here. What about joining me for dinner tonight?'

'I'd like that,' said Agatha, feeling her spirits soar. Damn Charles and James. She still had pulling power.

He said he would pick her up at her hotel at eight. 'I know a good place well outside of town,' he said.

Agatha walked back to the hotel with a light heart. She spent the rest of the day on her laptop, writing down everything about the case, and then she printed it all out on her portable printer to show to Patrick when he arrived.

Patrick turned up in the late afternoon. He settled down in Agatha's room and carefully studied her notes. He tapped a page. 'Is it possible this old boy, Archie Swale, might have murdered his ex-wife?'

'I feel doubtful about that. Charles appeared to think so.'

'We could drive over to Brighton this evening. I'd like to get a look at him.'

'He wouldn't see us. Besides, I've got a date.'

'Who?'

Agatha grinned. 'Just a fellow who picked me up.'

'Tell me about it.'

'Not like you to be so curious about my personal life. Oh, well. He bumped into me as I was coming out of M and S in the High Street. He apologized. He then said he recognized me from my photo in the local paper and wanted to hear all about my work. We had coffee and he's invited me out for dinner.'

'What does he do?'

'He's a builder. But a rich one. He's got a place in Marbella.'

'So have a lot of villains.'

'He's not a villain,' said Agatha hotly. 'Do you mean to say a man can't be attracted to me?'

She glared at him.

'No, no,' mumbled Patrick. 'When is he picking you up?'

'At eight o'clock.'

Patrick studied her flushed face in silence. Then he said, 'I'll run over to Brighton and wait outside this Swale's house. I'll get a better idea about him if I can see him.'

'How's Phil Marshall getting on?'

'He's amazing for his age. Never stops working. He says there's a newcomer in the village.'

'Who?'

'A widow called Deborah Fanshawe, hell-bent on chasing your ex.'

'What does she look like?'

'Phil says she's very attractive.'

I don't care any more, Agatha told herself fiercely. I've got a date. I'm moving on.

Agatha had gone out shopping again for her date. The dresses she had brought when she had expected to be going somewhere warm and glamorous were too filmy for this cold British summer. If anyone talks about global warming again, thought Agatha, I'll strike them.

She chose a white silk blouse with a plunging neckline and a black skirt cut on the bias. A pink pashmina completed the ensemble.

Agatha felt rejuvenated when she went down the stairs that evening to find Terry waiting for her. To her surprise, he was dressed in jeans, a donkey jacket and a plaid shirt.

'I'm overdressed,' said Agatha.

'You look great,' said Terry. 'I'm sorry I look like this, but I had to rush here from work. It's all right. They know me at the restaurant.'

Agatha had expected to be stepping into a Mercedes or a Rolls or some car like that, but there was a plain white van parked outside, just like the one Harry Beam used.

Her excitement about the evening was ebbing fast. If he were really interested, she thought, he would have made more of an effort.

He drove steadily out of town and up on to the windswept downs. 'We're going a long way,' said Agatha.

He smiled at her. 'It'll be worth it.'

Rain began to hammer against the windscreen.

The rubber had gone from one of the wipers and it made an irritating noise as it scraped backwards and forwards.

Finally he stopped. 'Here we are. Wait there and I'll open the door for you.'

'I should have brought an umbrella,' said Agatha. 'I'll be soaked before I get indoors.'

He moved round to the front of the car and then opened the passenger door.

'Out!' he said.

In the weak interior light of the car Agatha could plainly see he was holding a serviceable-looking revolver.

'What's this all about?' asked Agatha. 'Is this a joke?'

'Out!'

Wind and rain whipped Agatha's hair about her face. She peered this way and that looking for escape, but the revolver was now pressed into her side and urging her to the door of a low building.

Terry leaned round her and opened the door and prodded her in. He switched on an overhead light. Agatha found herself in a room empty except for one kitchen chair. Rain dripped through a crack in the ceiling. Despite her fear, she wondered why the electricity was working in such a derelict building.

'Sit down,' he barked.

Agatha sank down on to the hard chair. Her knees were trembling.

'Charlie said that only half the jewels were recovered. Where's the rest?'

'I don't know,' said Agatha. 'I really, truly, don't know. Why don't you ask Fred Jankers?' She suddenly remembered the items of jewellery Harry had found under the mattress.

'Charlie told me about you, how he overheard you blabbing.'

'Who are you?'

'Charlie worked for me. Why he had to go off on a sideline like armed robbery, I don't know. But I owe him a favour and I stick by my friends. He wants the rest of that jewellery for his missus.'

'A sideline? Marbella?' Agatha eyes widened. 'You're into something bigger. Drugs?'

He stared at her, his face hard and set. 'The jewellery,' he said. 'To refresh your memory, I'm going to start by shooting your kneecap.'

'Jankers has it,' said Agatha desperately. 'It's under the mattress in his home. He may not even have known it was there. Geraldine probably stashed it there.'

He lowered the revolver slightly. 'That's better. What was there?'

'I c-can't quite remember,' stammered Agatha. 'Two watches, gold chains, a sapphire-and-diamond necklace and I think there was a brooch.'

The revolver was raised again. 'Not enough. Where's the rest?'

'*I don't know!*' yelled Agatha, beside herself with fright.

He levelled the gun at her kneecap. Agatha closed her eyes.

And then a stentorian voice outside yelled, 'The building is surrounded. Come out with your hands up!'

Terry switched out the light. She could hear him moving off to the back of the building. Agatha got to her feet. Blue light was now flooding in the window. She crept towards the door, opened it and dashed out into the rain. A policeman seized her and hustled her off to a police car.

Armed policemen then rushed into the building. Agatha heard a tap on the window of the police car and looked out. Patrick Mulligan stood there. She lowered the window.

'I thought I'd better follow you,' said Patrick. 'I didn't like the idea of you being picked up by a complete stranger.'

'Thanks, Patrick. You've saved my life.'

'I'd like to get in out of this rain. I'm soaked.'

Agatha moved over and Patrick climbed in beside her. 'Did you call them when you saw him with that gun?' asked Agatha. 'They got here quickly.'

'I decided to call them when I saw him heading out into open country. To be on the safe side, I said you had been kidnapped and that he was armed. Good thing for me it turned out to be true.'

Agatha shivered. 'What's going on out there? Have they got him?'

'I don't know, but I'm so wet I'd rather wait in here and find out.'

The car door opened. 'I am Detective Chief

Superintendent Willerby of the Sussex CID. It's time we had a talk, Mrs Raisin.'

'Have you got him?'

'Not yet. There seems to have been some escape route through the cellar. My men are out on the downs and we've sent for the dogs. We'll get him soon. I'd like you to come over to my car. You too, Mr Mulligan.'

They went out into the rain and followed him to his car. He got in the front beside his driver. Agatha and Patrick slid into the back. Agatha was grateful that the car engine was on and the heater was running.

'Tell me from the beginning,' ordered Willerby.

So Agatha did, feeling sillier by the minute that she had allowed a complete stranger to pick her up in the middle of an investigation.

When she had finished, he made a phone call. Agatha started to speak again, but he held up his hand for silence. Whoever he had phoned answered, because he said, 'I thought that might be the case,' and rang off.

He turned back to Agatha. 'We don't have the name Terry Armstrong on our records, so we'll take you to headquarters at Lewes and you can look at mug shots and then give the police artist a description. Now, you, Mr Mulligan. What prompted you to follow her?'

'Just seemed strange, this chap turning up out of nowhere. I didn't like it, so I thought I'd follow and see where they went.'

'But you must have phoned before they got to that derelict cottage because you then phoned back later and gave us the location. Fortunately, we were already on our way.'

'I couldn't get close for a while in case he caught on to the fact that someone was following him, so I took a chance and switched off my lights. At one point he stopped,' lied Patrick, 'and I saw he was holding a gun to her head.'

'Wait here,' said Willerby, and he got out of the car.

And so they did – waited and waited while gusts of wind rocked the car and rain slashed against the windows.

Agatha fell into an uneasy sleep and soon Patrick fell asleep as well.

When Agatha awoke, the wind had died down and the rain had stopped. Patrick had woken up too.

'I need to pee,' said Agatha. She leaned forward to the driver. 'Can I go back into that cottage and see if there's a loo?'

'No, the forensics are working there now. You'll need to find a bush.'

Agatha got out of the car and looked around in the darkness. She saw a clump of bushes and went behind it, crouched down and lowered the flimsy knickers that she had put on in the hope of a hot date.

She relieved herself and was reaching for her knickers when she saw two green eyes staring at her. She let out a scream of terror and tried to dart from the bushes, but her knickers were caught round her ankles and she fell headlong.

Two policemen appeared with torches. 'Was that him?' one cried.

'Two eyes were staring at me,' gasped Agatha.

At that moment, a fox slid past them in the light of the torches and disappeared. 'There are your green eyes,' said one policeman.

He helped Agatha to her feet. She bent down and pulled her knickers up. She felt like crying with shame. She, who liked to appear the tough woman detective, had gone out on a date with a man she did not know and nearly got herself killed and now she had been terrified out of her wits by a fox.

As the policemen moved off, she distinctly heard one mutter to the other, 'Silly cow.'

Agatha got back in beside Patrick. 'Don't ask,' she said.

She fell asleep again and did not awaken until a pale dawn was streaking the sky.

Willerby came back at last, looking cross and exhausted. 'How he got away is beyond me. Yes, there was an underground route out from the cellar, but we've had dogs and men out covering the downs and there's not a trace of him. We'll get back to headquarters and take your statement.'

Next morning, Charles Fraith switched on the television set he kept at the end of the dining table before settling down to his breakfast. His guests, Guy and Cynthia Partington, were still asleep.

More trouble in Iraq, more suicide bombs, and then the announcer said, 'We have a newsflash.

137

Woman detective Agatha Raisin, who is at Snoth-on-Sea investigating the murder of Geraldine Jankers, who was found strangled on the beach, was kidnapped last night by an armed gunman. She was rescued by police. According to police reports, the gunman was using the name Terry Armstrong. More later.'

Charles sat transfixed, his knife and fork hovering over his plate. Agatha would never forgive him for leaving her in the lurch. He felt he ought to get back to Snoth-on-Sea immediately, but he had a week's entertainment lined up for his guests.

Unaware of Agatha's drama, James Lacey finally switched off his computer that morning and walked along to the general stores. Deborah Fanshawe seemed to appear from nowhere and fell into step beside him.

'Lovely morning,' she said cheerfully.

'Where did you spring from?' asked James, because Lilac Lane, where he and Agatha had their cottages, was a dead end.

'Oh, walking in the fields,' she said vaguely. 'We haven't really had a chance to get properly acquainted.' The sun glinted on her masses of brown hair. Her long legs under a short skirt were much in evidence. 'Why don't you drop round my place, say, at eight this evening, and I'll cook dinner?'

James hesitated. Then he smiled. He felt he

needed something to take his mind off abandoning Agatha. 'That would be nice.'

'See you, then.' She waggled her fingers at him and strode off.

James walked on to the village shop. He was just picking up a basket when Miss Simms rushed up to him. 'Isn't it terrible about our Agatha?' she gasped.

He stared down at her. 'What? What's happened?'

'It was on the morning news. She was captured by an armed gunman and the police had to rescue her!'

James dropped the basket and rushed back home. He switched on a twenty-four-hour news service and waited impatiently. At last the news item he wanted came up on the screen. There was a brief account of the kidnapping and the search over the downs for the armed gunman. There was film of Agatha and Patrick leaving the police station. Agatha looked terrible.

'You're what?' demanded the vicar.

'I'm just going to take the car and drive down to Snoth-on-Sea. I feel Mrs Raisin needs me.'

'I forbid you to go. That woman is trouble, has always been trouble, and I don't want you involved in it,' raged the vicar.

Mrs Bloxby pushed a strand of grey hair from her face. There was an unfamiliar edge in her voice as she said, 'I am going, Alf, and that is all there is to it.'

'What about the parish duties?'

Mrs Bloxby had been packing a travelling bag. 'The parish can do without me for a couple of days. When did we last have a holiday?'

'What's that got to do with it?'

'Just that Mrs Raisin needs me and I need a change of scene. There is enough food in the deep freeze to keep you going. Stop looming over me, dear.'

'But I need the car!'

'There is a perfectly good bicycle in the shed. Stop fussing.'

Deborah Fanshawe returned later that day with a pile of groceries. She set about preparing an elaborate meal, smiling as she thought of Agatha Raisin. From the village gossip she had regarded Agatha as competition. That was until the previous evening, when she had seen a group photo of the Carsely Ladies' Society and Agatha had been pointed out to her. Really, the woman was no competition at all. She was short and stocky and had funny little eyes.

Deborah suddenly noticed a red light on her phone was flashing, indicating she had a message.

She picked up the phone and listened impatiently to the British Telecom voice saying she had one message and if she wanted to hear it, to press one. She pressed one and found herself listening to James Lacey's voice. 'Deborah, I am so sorry I must cancel this evening. My friend

Agatha is in trouble and I must go and see if I can help. I'll phone you when I get back.'

Deborah slowly put down the phone. Then she ran out of her cottage and down through the village to Lilac Lane. Curtains at cottage windows twitched. Elderly voices marvelled she could run so fast in such high heels.

She arrived breathless and panting at James's cottage. She rang the bell and hammered on the door. No reply. Then she turned slowly around. His car had gone. She simply could not understand it. What had this Agatha Raisin got to offer that she hadn't?

Agatha, finally released by the police, slept most of the day in her bedroom with the door locked and a chair propped under the handle. If only the police had caught Terry or whatever his name was. She was terrified that he might come back looking for her. She had not thought she would be able to sleep, but when she woke, it was early evening and the phone was ringing.

It was. Patrick. 'I've just come back from the police station. They got fingerprints from the cottage. Terry Armstrong is actually Brian McNally. He's wanted by Interpol for drug dealing and for murder.'

'There's an extradition treaty with Spain,' said Agatha. 'He said he had a place in Marbella.'

'Interpol's checking that. If he has, he won't dare go near it. All ports and airports are being watched. There's something else.'

'What?'

'Mrs Bloxby's just arrived.'

'Oh, that's marvellous. Send her up.'

Agatha got out of bed and scrambled into her clothes. But when there was a knock at the door, she asked cautiously, 'Who is it?'

'Mrs Bloxby.'

Agatha removed the chair and unlocked the door. She felt she had never before been more delighted to look into the mild grey eyes of her friend.

'Come in. You shouldn't have come all this way, but it's marvellous to see you!'

Mrs Bloxby came in carrying her bag. 'I haven't had time to check in yet,' she said.

'You must let me pay for your room. Wasn't your husband furious at you going?'

'He will miss me because of the parish duties, but he can manage for a couple of days. Now tell me everything that has happened.'

'I'm hungry,' said Agatha. 'The food here's turned out not bad and at the moment I don't feel brave enough to risk leaving the hotel. If I eat something, I'll get my courage back. After that, we'll check you in.'

Mrs Bloxby was a good listener. She had years of practice from listening patiently to parish complaints.

The evening grew dark outside as Agatha talked and spray from the rising waves hammered against the windows.

'It's interesting,' said Mrs Bloxby when Agatha had finally finished and coffee was being served.

'Which part?'

'Well, the husbands.'

'Which ones?'

'Archie Swale and Fred Jankers.'

'What about them?'

'I was just wondering if either of them had a record.'

'The police said nothing to me.'

'They wouldn't. You see, I think a noisy, coarse sort of woman like Geraldine Jankers would like criminals.'

'But as far as I gather, she was after money. She pretended to be all meek and mild before her weddings.'

'Still, I have found in the parish that battered wives who are finally persuaded to leave their husbands somehow manage to find another one the same. Mrs Jankers may have thought she was simply after the money, but there might have been something villainous there which subconsciously attracted her. Take Mrs Prissy Burford, for example.'

'That odd little woman who lives up Back Lane?'

'The same. Now, before you arrived in the village, she was married to Paul Burford, a raving alcoholic. She had a terrible time with him. Then he joined Alcoholics Anonymous and the change was miraculous and we were all so happy for her. But she divorced him and took up with a much younger man and he drank like a fish. If he hadn't left her, she'd still be with him.'

Agatha saw Patrick entering the dining room and waved to him. 'I hope there's some food left,' he said, sitting down with them.

Agatha told him about Mrs Bloxby's idea and Patrick said he would walk along to the police station after he had eaten. 'That is, when the tide goes down,' he said. 'It's getting dangerous out there. A chunk of masonry fell off one of the buildings on the front, they say, and still the council will do nothing about it.'

Mrs Bloxby and Agatha said goodnight to him. Agatha waited while Mrs Bloxby was checked into a hotel room, and was delighted to find the room next to her own was available.

'I thought the hotel would be full of press,' said Agatha to Nick Loncar, the receptionist.

'It was, but some big story broke over in Brighton and they all rushed off.'

Agatha sat up late into the night, going over her notes. She jumped nervously when her phone rang and looked at her watch. Two in the morning. She gingerly picked up the receiver.

'It's James here, Agatha,' said that once-loved voice. 'I've arrived.'

Chapter Eight

'James,' said Agatha faintly. 'What are you doing here at this time of night?'

'I thought I'd better come,' he said awkwardly.

Agatha pulled herself together. 'I'll see you tomorrow – if I have time.' She put down the receiver.

James stared at the dead phone. He felt he should have apologized. Maybe tomorrow.

Agatha switched off her computer. She thought she should be feeling some sort of excitement over the fact that James had come back, but all she knew was that she was suddenly very tired.

She undressed and crawled into bed. Her last waking thought was a hope that Charles was having a miserable time.

James was taken aback when he entered the dining room next morning for breakfast to find Mrs Bloxby placidly tucking into a plate of bacon and eggs. He was very surprised to see her and then surprised again by the fact that

Mrs Bloxby did not seem in the least surprised to see *him*.

'Why are you here?' he asked, joining her.

'For the same reason as you, Mr Lacey. Agatha needs all the support she can get. I knocked on her door before I came down. She will be joining us shortly.'

James felt guilty and uncomfortable. When Agatha walked into the dining room he jumped to his feet and pulled out a chair for her. Mrs Bloxby had just finished her bacon and eggs and wondered for a moment whether to leave them, but Agatha looked fresh and brisk, and not at all flustered by the presence of her ex-husband.

'I'm waiting to hear from Patrick,' said Agatha. 'He's checking out your theory, Mrs Bloxby.'

'What theory's that?' asked James.

Agatha's bearlike eyes turned on him, cool and efficient. It's as if I'm now a stranger, thought James. Agatha described how Mrs Bloxby had thought that the two ex-husbands might have something criminal in their backgrounds.

Under her apparent calm, Agatha was privately praying that the gunman, Brian McNally, had gone back to Spain, or anywhere out of the country for that matter, and would not come back to try to assault her again.

Outside the long windows of the dining room the day was bright and sunny. James and Agatha ordered breakfast. Mrs Bloxby decided to withdraw tactfully to another table, assuming James would want to make some sort of apology, if he had not done so already.

'So what's the plan for today?' asked James.

'I think your plan for the day should be to go back to Carsely,' said Agatha.

'I suppose you must be upset with me –'

'*Upset* with you? That's putting it mildly. Anyway, it doesn't matter now. I can do without you lurking around and getting under my feet.'

James's face flamed with temper. 'You should be grateful, yes *grateful*, that I am here to protect you.'

'I have Patrick. You weren't around when I was being kidnapped. Fat lot of good you were. Eat your breakfast and stop staring at me.'

'I did nothing wrong,' said James stiffly. 'We were supposed to be going on holiday together, but you changed your mind, not me. I was very angry with you, but I have forgiven you.'

'Were you always such a pompous prat, or have I just begun to realize it?' said Agatha, stabbing her fork into a poached egg. 'Oh, thank goodness, here's Patrick.'

'It's been interesting,' said Patrick. 'Any hope of breakfast?'

'Sure.' Agatha signalled to the waitress. She waited impatiently while Patrick gave his order. 'Well?'

'Minor stuff. Fred Jankers once set fire to his school. Served time in a juvenile offenders' hostel. Nothing that anyone knows since then.'

'What about Archie Swale?'

'When he was serving in Northern Ireland with the paras – he was a corporal – he attacked one of the soldiers in a drunken rage. Spent some time in the glasshouse, but not discharged from the army.'

'Be back in a minute,' said Agatha. 'I'll just tell Mrs Bloxby to join us. She should hear this.'

When Mrs Bloxby returned, Agatha said, 'You're such a shrewd judge of character. I would like you to get a look at both Jankers and Swale.'

'I'd better try to do that today. I promised my husband I would be back tomorrow. He telephoned me this morning.'

'I'll drive you to Brighton,' said Agatha. 'We can park outside his house and when he leaves you can get a look at him. Good. There's Fred Jankers just coming in. I'll take you over and introduce you.'

Agatha is going on as if she's forgotten my very existence, thought James.

Agatha introduced Mrs Bloxby to Fred Jankers. Mrs Bloxby began to talk in her soothing voice about how sorry she was to hear of his wife's death. Agatha made an excuse and left her to it.

'I'm going up to my room to make some calls,' said James, getting to his feet.

'You do that,' replied Agatha.

'What's going on with you and your ex?' asked Patrick.

Agatha was suddenly furious. 'He said it was my fault he had gone off and left me.'

'I always thought he was a confirmed bachelor,' said Patrick. 'Anyway, what do you want me to do now?'

'I'd like you to come with me and Mrs Bloxby to have a look at Swale. I think he's too old and frail to have committed such a violent murder, but I'd like to see what you think.'

Upstairs in his room, James paced up and down. He had been so sure that Agatha would treat his arrival with gladness and relief. And he had turned down a dinner with a very attractive woman. He fished in his pocket and riffled through some cards until he found Deborah's.

His ego was bruised. It was just that the adoring Agatha had previously always been there in his life. Perhaps he had vaguely thought, forgetting the disaster of their marriage, that they would settle down together at some point.

James decided that he should really phone Deborah and apologize properly for having rushed off. It never dawned on him that a proper apology to Agatha would have mended fences.

He dialled her number. 'Deborah?'

'James, darling,' she cooed. 'How nice of you to call. Where are you?'

'Snoth-on-Sea.'

'What a funny name! And how is Mrs Raisin?'

'Detecting as usual. I really shouldn't have come. I thought she would be shattered after her experience, but she's as tough as old boots. The reason I phoned was to apologize for having dashed off like that.'

'Don't worry. We can make it another night. When are you coming back?'

James hesitated. He was the one who had worked on cases with Agatha in the past. He had a sudden desire to find out something that would impress her.

'Maybe another day or two,' he said. 'I'll phone you when I get back.'

Deborah replaced the receiver and sat at her kitchen table deep in thought. Her cottage was decorated in what she fondly considered to be true country style, with chintz and horse brasses and bunches of herbs hanging from hooks on the kitchen ceiling. She had just been beginning to wonder why she had buried herself in the country when she had come across James Lacey and had decided she wanted to marry him.

She had invited several of the members of the ladies' society for dinner that evening, but as she looked around the piles of ingredients spread about her kitchen, she wished she hadn't bothered. Deborah was strictly a colour-supplement cook. She specialized in recipes that demanded a whole string of totally unnecessary herbs.

She had bagged her previous husband after a ruthless campaign, forgetting that it was that very ruthlessness of hers which had eventually made him ask for a divorce.

At last she picked up the phone again and rang all the women she had invited and cancelled the dinner. Then she got out a road atlas and searched it until she found Snoth-on-Sea. She conjured up a mental image of Agatha Raisin based on that group photograph. No competition at all, she told herself.

As they drove to Brighton, Mrs Bloxby gave her impressions of Fred Jankers. 'It's hard to tell. He seems very quiet and gentlemanly. Quite old-fashioned, and yet he is only in his fifties. But it could be an act he's perfected. You say Mrs Jankers married him for his money? Perhaps it might have been the other way around. Was she rich?'

'I don't know,' said Agatha.

'It would also be interesting to find out how his businesses are doing and whether he insured her life.'

'Good point,' said Patrick. 'I'd better get on to that when we get back.'

Agatha felt suddenly tired. All her bright hard efficiency seemed to be draining away and, horror of horrors, deep down she felt the beginnings of that old longing for James. He had looked as handsome as ever that morning with his bright blue eyes, tanned face and dark hair going grey at the temples.

They parked outside Archie Swale's house in Brighton and waited. 'Maybe he's gone out already?' suggested Patrick after an hour.

'I know,' said Mrs Bloxby. 'I'll go and knock at the door and say I'm collecting for something. I've had years of practice.'

'Be careful,' warned Agatha as the vicar's wife got out of the car.

Mrs Bloxby went across the road and knocked at the door. When Archie answered it, she gave him a sweet smile and said, 'I am collecting for Help the Aged and wondered whether you could spare anything.'

'I can give you a pound.'

'That would be marvellous.'

'You'd better come in. I emptied the change out of my trousers last night and left it on the desk.'

She followed him into his sitting room. He went to his desk and picked up a pound. Mrs Bloxby opened her handbag and produced a sticker from a previous Help the Aged collection from a number of other old charity stickers.

'No sticker,' he said. 'I had a good suede jacket ruined by one of those. Must be hard on the feet, all this collecting.'

'It is, rather.'

'I say, would you like a sherry?'

'Why, that is very kind of you.'

'Are you married?'

'Yes, my husband is the vicar of . . . Saint Edmund's,' said Mrs Bloxby, privately praying that there was a Saint Edmund's in Brighton.

He handed her a small glass of sherry. Mrs Bloxby looked across at the regimental photograph. 'I see you are an army man.'

'Was. I miss it. Too old for it now.'

'This government does seem very determined to merge the old regiments.'

A tide of angry red suffused his face. 'Bunch of Commie bastards. Lefties. Faggots. I'd shoot the lot of them! I'm sorry. I shouldn't have said that.'

'It's all right. We still have free speech in this country. Or do we?'

He went off on another rant while Mrs Bloxby sipped her sherry and covertly studied him. She noticed he had very powerful wrists.

Feeling she had heard enough, Mrs Bloxby waited until he had paused for breath, and said, 'I really must be on my way.'

He looked disappointed. 'Call again any time,' he said, ushering her to the door.

He was standing on the front step watching her leave, so Mrs Bloxby walked right past the car where Agatha and Patrick were crouched down and out of the square. Agatha only cautiously raised her head when she heard the street door slam. She drove out of the square and caught up with Mrs Bloxby.

'How did you get on?' she asked when Mrs Bloxby had climbed into the car.

'I got an impression of a violent, angry man. He has powerful wrists. I think he has high blood pressure. He looks too old to have committed a murder and yet I feel he could have found great strength in one of his bursts of rage.'

'What was he raging about?'

'The government.'

'Well, I rage about them myself.'

'Not like this. Quite beside himself. If I am to make myself useful, perhaps I should try to engineer a further conversation with Mr Jankers before I leave.'

Agatha checked the clock on the dashboard. 'Nearly lunchtime. He'll probably be in the dining room.'

'Such a big breakfast,' sighed Mrs Bloxby. 'But I will see what I can do.'

When they returned to the hotel a policeman was waiting to escort Agatha and Patrick back to police headquarters in Lewes for more questioning about the hunt for Brian McNally.

Mrs Bloxby retreated to her room to telephone her husband to assure him she would be returning home as soon as possible and then she descended to the dining room. There was no sign of Fred Jankers. She walked through to the bar and found him ensconced in a chair by the window.

Mrs Bloxby approached him. 'Do you mind if I join you? I always feel rather self-conscious drinking on my own.'

'Please do. Let me buy you a drink. What'll it be?'

'Just an orange juice, thank you.'

'Nothing stronger?'

'No, orange juice will do fine. I am thirsty.'

Fred ordered her drink. 'I never asked you,' he said. 'Are you a detective as well?'

'Oh, no, Mr Jankers. I am married to the vicar of the village where I and Mrs Raisin both live. I heard about the terrible attack on her and thought she might need some help.'

'So you came all this way? Wish I had friends like you.'

'You must miss your wife terribly,' said Mrs Bloxby in her quiet soothing voice.

'Here's your orange juice. Cheers. Well, fact is, after I got over the awful shock of her being murdered and all, I felt a bit relieved. Is that wicked?'

'I gather you did not know her very long.'

'No, unfortunately. I hate to shock a lady like yourself, but I think Geraldine was after my money.'

'How dreadful for you. How did you find out?'

'Just after we were married. I overheard her talking to that Cyril Hammond, a friend of hers. He's still in the hotel. I heard her saying, "I know Fred's not much to look at, but there should be some rich pickings." That's all I heard.'

'I cannot help wondering,' said Mrs Bloxby, 'why a lady such as your late wife would go down to the beach in the middle of the night. I mean, she cannot have known anything about the tides and it's a dangerous place to go.'

'I think she was plotting something,' said Fred. He ran one podgy hand nervously over his head.

'Like what?'

'Maybe plotting to kill me.'

'My dear Mr Jankers!'

'She made me take out a heavy insurance policy, and if she was plotting with anyone it would be that old friend of hers, Cyril Hammond.

'Have you told the police this?'

'I tried, but Cyril says he was asleep and his wife backs him up.'

'Mr Jankers, have you not considered leaving here? I am sure the police would allow you to go.'

'Fact is, I think the answer to that murder is here. Mind you, that friend of yours doesn't strike me as much of a detective.'

'Oh, she is very good. She never lets a case go until she has an answer.'

Could this man have murdered his wife? wondered Mrs Bloxby. He seemed too quiet and neat in his business suit.

'Time to eat,' said Fred. 'Care to join me?'

But Mrs Bloxby felt she had done enough for Agatha. 'I really must go upstairs and pack,' she said, rising to her feet.

He rose as well. A magazine which had been half hidden by his bottom fell to the floor. He whipped it up and put it behind his back, but not before Mrs Bloxby had seen the lurid cover and the title, *Hot Tits*.

Mrs Bloxby felt suddenly tired as she walked along the long corridor to her room. How eerie this old hotel was, she thought, with all those empty rooms.

A maid was just coming out of Agatha's room, which was next to her own. The woman ducked her head by way of greeting and hurried off along the corridor. Mrs Bloxby's eyes narrowed in suspicion. The maid had not been carrying any cleaning materials.

She unlocked the door of her own room and went in. She phoned the manager. 'I have just seen a maid coming out of Mrs Raisin's room. She was wearing a blue overall. She was thin and sallow with black hair. Do you have a maid like that on your staff?'

'Doesn't fit the description of anyone I've got,' said Mr Beeston.

Mrs Bloxby thanked him and then phoned the local police station and asked to be put through to Detective Inspector Barret. When he came on the line, she told him about the suspicious maid.

He said he would be right along.

When he arrived, Mr Beeston supplied the pass key, and Barret, followed by Mrs Bloxby, went into Agatha's room. Nothing appeared to have been disturbed. 'I'll get someone along to check for fingerprints,' said Barret. 'Mrs Raisin is at headquarters in Lewes. I'll phone there and tell her when she's returned not to go up to her room until we're finished.'

'That's new,' said Mrs Bloxby, noticing a tray containing a flask, a jug of milk, sugar bowl and plate of biscuits on the table by the window.

'We'll check that as well,' said Barret.

James Lacey went out for a long walk that day. He missed working with Agatha. He felt he would really need to sit down with her and have a long talk. He had finally accepted that he would have to apologize.

He returned to the hotel in the early evening, hurrying to beat the high tide which was already sending waves smashing into the sea wall.

Agatha was sitting in the reception area, looking tired and wan. Patrick was with her.

'How are things going?' asked James.

Agatha told him briefly about the suspect maid and ended by saying, 'They're still working on my room.'

'Might I have a word with you in private, Agatha?'

Patrick started to get to his feet. 'It's all right,' said James. 'I'll take Agatha into the bar.'

Cyril Hammond and his wife Dawn were in the bar. Not for the first time Agatha wondered why they did not go home. They waved to Agatha to join them, but she called, 'Later.'

She and James settled in a corner of the bar away from the Hammonds.

James ordered drinks and then leaned forward. He took Agatha's hands in his and her treacherous heart began to thump.

'Agatha . . . dearest,' he began.

And then a voice called, 'Coo-ee, James. It's me!'

Deborah Fanshawe sank down in a vacant chair next to James. 'I thought I would give you a nice surprise,' she said. 'What a dismal hole this place is! But it was the least I could do, considering you missed my splendid dinner.'

Agatha rose to her feet.

'Where are you going?' asked James.

'I'm buggering off to where I'm wanted,' said Agatha savagely.

Mrs Bloxby had joined Patrick when Agatha stormed back into the reception area. She looked at Agatha's hurt and angry face and said sympathetically, 'I believe Mrs Fanshawe has arrived.'

'Let's talk about something else,' said Agatha, jerking a chair forward and sitting down.

'Mrs Bloxby has found out something interesting,' said Patrick. 'Fred Jankers was reading a porno magazine.'

'Him and every other blasted man in this country, I should think,' said Agatha.

'Please listen,' urged Mrs Bloxby.

'When I was in the force,' said Patrick, 'we once employed a profiler to see if we could find out the identity of a rapist in the Mircester area. He said that rapists often have an abused childhood and start with torturing animals and then a bit of arson and often then proceed to sex crimes. Now we know our Fred set fire to his school. It would be interesting to find out if there are any unsolved cases of rape in the Lewisham area.'

'That would take forever,' grumbled Agatha, 'and we don't have the resources of the police. Let's eat.'

They went into the dining room. 'I must leave first thing in the morning,' said Mrs Bloxby.

159

James and Deborah entered the dining room and sat at another table. Agatha scowled horribly.

After a while Mrs Bloxby said gently, 'Deborah is laughing and flirting, but Mr Lacey looks miserable.'

'Don't care,' said Agatha sulkily, poking at her food with her fork.

Barret walked in and joined them. 'You can go back to your room now. We're finished there.'

'Any results?'

'Yes. We got a quick result on fingerprints. The woman who went into your room is Candice Skirisky, a Bulgarian. She's a mule.'

The lyrics of 'Would You Like to Swing on a Star' danced through Agatha's brain.

'A mule?'

'One of those women who are drug carriers. She was arrested a few years ago. The police had a tip-off and she was arrested at Heathrow. She had swallowed packages of cocaine. She said she was to be paid two thousand pounds, but when she went to a hotel room in Sofia to meet this man, he told her she would be paid according to how many cocaine packages she could swallow. She was told that when she arrived in London she would be met by another man who would give her a laxative, retrieve the drugs and pay her. But she would not reveal any names. She said the man had told her that if she revealed any names, she would be killed. We think maybe Brian McNally got hold of her.'

'What was in that flask?' asked Agatha.

'We're still analysing the contents. We are putting two policemen on guard at this hotel.'

'Maybe Mrs Raisin should go home,' suggested Patrick.

'We need her here,' said Barret, 'and she would be safer here with the police guarding the place.'

'If this Brian McNally is a powerful drug baron and can command people like this woman to try to murder me – that's if there turns out to be something sinister in that flask of coffee,' said Agatha, 'then surely he could command someone to murder Geraldine Jankers if he thought she had double-crossed a member of his gang.'

'We're looking at that angle.'

'The thing that puzzles me,' said Patrick, 'is why was the haul of jewels from a Lewisham jeweller so valuable? I mean, it's hardly Cartier or Tiffany's.'

'Benson and Judge, the jeweller's, is an old-established firm. Their main showroom is in Mayfair. They had moved a quantity of their best items down to Lewisham for an exhibition for a children's charity. All the local worthies were to be invited. The robbery took place a day before the party.'

'Why wasn't the stuff fenced right away?' asked Agatha.

'I think Charlie Black had managed to stash it all before he was arrested. I think he planned to fence it when he got out and then found it had disappeared.'

Barret got to his feet. 'I'll be off. I'll call on you tomorrow.'

He looked across the dining room. 'Isn't that Mr Lacey who was here with you during the murder?'

'Yes,' said Agatha curtly.

'Who's that woman with him?'

'The village tart,' said Agatha savagely.

'I see.' Barret looked down at Agatha with a glint of humour in his eyes.

When he had left, Mrs Bloxby said gently, 'Would you like me to stay in your room tonight, Mrs Raisin?'

'It's all right,' said Agatha. 'I know you are right next door. Or rather, the new next door. I changed our rooms and got your stuff moved into the new one.'

'I shall be leaving before breakfast.'

'I'll look after her,' said Patrick.

They finished their meal and left the dining room, Agatha avoiding looking at James.

James Lacey was feeling hunted. Deborah should never have come. She did not seem to notice his silence but chattered on about the iniquities of her ex-husband and all the men who had tried to sleep with her.

At last, when she paused for breath, he said, 'Look, Deborah, it's like this. I was about to have some sort of reconciliation with Agatha and you arrived at precisely the wrong minute.'

Deborah's mouth fell open in surprise. 'But why?'

'I am very fond of her still.'

Deborah's eyes narrowed. 'You are a very silly man. I thought we had something going.'

'You must be mad. I've barely spoken to you before this evening.'

Deborah burst into tears. She had fantasized so much about him on the journey down that she was sure they would be in bed together before the night was out.

James waited until she had finished crying and then said quietly, 'You must see you have made a mistake. You had better go home.'

He rose and left the dining room and nearly collided with Cyril Hammond and his wife. As he walked away, James wondered what the couple were doing staying on. He wondered whether to go straight to Agatha's room and try to explain things but then decided to leave it until the morning.

Chapter Nine

Charles Fraith was not feeling guilty at having abandoned Agatha. But he was bored. He could not understand why his friends, Cynthia and Guy Partington, had suddenly decided to cut short their visit. It did not occur to him that on the two occasions when Charles had invited the Partingtons out for dinner, he appeared to have forgotten his wallet.

He knew if he went back to join Agatha she would be very angry with him, but she had been angry before and had come round. It was worth a try. The previously dull summer weather had worsened and sheets of rain were making lakes on the lawn outside his windows.

Agatha slept soundly that night because when she had changed her room and Mrs Bloxby's, she had demanded ones which did not overlook the sea, having become tired of the sinister roar of the waves at high tide.

She awoke in the morning feeling stronger than she had felt since the discovery of the fake maid. She wondered if they had found out yet if there had been anything sinister in that flask and then remembered that it seemed to be only on fictional forensic detective programmes on television that results came through immediately.

Mrs Bloxby knocked on her door and came in to say goodbye. 'I wouldn't worry about Mrs Fanshawe,' she said. 'Such a pushy sort of woman. Mr Lacey won't like that at all.'

'Don't care,' muttered Agatha, but she could not help wondering what James had been about to say to her before the awful Fanshawe woman had breezed into the bar.

'I must leave now,' said Mrs Bloxby. 'Do take care of yourself.'

'I'll try. Give my love to Carsely.'

'I'll do that and I'll make sure your cats are being well looked after.'

Agatha's cleaner always looked after Agatha's pets when she was away somewhere.

As she walked down the stairs with her friend, Agatha wondered what on earth she could do that day. Then she thought of the Hammonds. It was time to ask that pair just why they were staying on.

She walked Mrs Bloxby round to the car park, waved goodbye and then walked slowly back to the hotel.

Agatha joined Patrick in the dining room. There was no sign of either Deborah or James. Agatha thought of those long legs of Deborah's and had a sudden awful mental picture of them

165

wrapped around James's neck. She shrugged to dispel the image.

'Going to rain,' said Patrick. 'Big black clouds creeping in across the sea. What's the programme for today?'

'I think we have to hang around the hotel. The police will be back with more questions and I'd better be available. Have you seen James?'

'Not yet.'

'I want to have a go at the Hammonds. Cyril knew Geraldine for a long time. He knew Charlie Black. I wonder if there's anything criminal in *his* record.'

'Trouble is, my contact at the police station is getting a bit tired of me using him. Maybe I'll try later, take him a bottle of Scotch or something.'

'Okay, put it down on your expenses.'

'The gentlemen of the press were round earlier. There must have been a leak.'

'I'll tell the manager to keep them outside the hotel.'

'Are you sure? In the first place, I already suggested to Beeston that he ban the press, but he says he can do with the custom. Also, a bit of publicity never hurt anyone. Hold a press conference. Hint that you are nearly about to expose the murderer of Geraldine.'

'I suppose I could do that. Is my hair all right? Maybe I should find a hairdresser.'

'I wouldn't bother. Look. It's started to bucket.'

Sheets of rain were being driven against the long windows of the dining room.

'Oh Lord,' muttered Agatha. 'Here comes the femme fatale of Carsely.'

Deborah marched up to them. 'Where's James?'

'Blessed if I know,' said Agatha.

'He's not in his room.'

'He's probably gone out for a walk. Why don't you go and hunt him down?'

'I'll need to fix my hair first.'

Deborah strode off. 'That's the first time I've seen a mini-raincoat,' said Patrick. 'Still, I suppose she knows she's got good legs.'

Agatha, who prided herself on her own good legs, gave him a sour look. But she was comforted by the fact that James was not hanging around Deborah.

They fell silent, Agatha already missing the comforting presence of Mrs Bloxby and Patrick wondering whether a bottle of whisky would elicit any information from his contact. At times like this he wished he were in his old job with access to computer records and the right to interview anyone he felt like.

'Tide's coming up,' said Patrick at last. 'If it's as bad as this now, God help the residents of Snoth when the autumn gales start.' Through the open door of the dining room he saw Deborah leaving again, carrying a large golf umbrella under her arm. He half rose.

'Where are you going?' asked Agatha.

'I've just seen Deborah heading out. I should warn her it isn't safe.'

'Oh, sit down. Let the silly cow get a soaking.'

A high wind had got up and the rain was streaming down. Deborah unfurled her large umbrella. She hesitated. Waves were crashing over the sea wall.

But in the distance, heading towards the hotel, through the rain and waves, she could see James Lacey.

Deborah smiled. He could not really have meant all those things he had said to her. She had been successful in the hunt before by never taking no for an answer. She would run towards him. She saw it all in slow motion in her head as if on a film.

She started to run. Patrick, who had risen and was watching her through the windows, shouted, 'Stop!'

'Stop what?' asked Agatha, lighting a cigarette.

Patrick ran for the door.

Deborah clutched her umbrella. The wind seemed to be buffeting from every direction. And then she saw James turning off into the shelter of a side street. He hadn't even seen her! She ploughed on, water now swirling about her feet, deafened by the roar of the waves.

Patrick, shouting and yelling, watched in horror as a great gust of wind caught under the umbrella and dragged her to the edge of the sea wall. Ducking and weaving, he ran towards her.

One great grey wave curled over the sea wall and like some gigantic hand caught Deborah.

One minute she was there and the next she had gone.

Patrick was no swimmer and he knew that even if he were, the waves would batter him against the wall. He retreated to shelter and called the emergency services. He felt sick.

Agatha looked up as Patrick, dripping wet, walked slowly into the dining room. 'What's up?' she asked.

'It's Deborah. She's gone.'

'Good riddance.'

'No, Agatha. I mean she's really gone. A great wave dragged her over the wall and into the sea.'

'Have you phoned the lifeboat?'

'Called the emergency services. They'll get everyone out.'

'This is terrible. I didn't like the woman, but I certainly didn't wish her dead.' Agatha had turned pale. She was beginning to feel this seaside resort had some sort of curse on it.

'I'd better go up to my room and dry myself,' said Patrick. 'Here come the Hammonds.'

They came up to Agatha's table. 'Mind if we join you? It's ages since we've had a chat.'

'Sit down,' said Agatha, 'although I don't feel much like chatting. Someone from our village, Deborah Fanshawe, has just been swept out to sea.'

'You mean the cracker with legs up to her armpits?' asked Cyril.

'Yes.'

'That's awful. She'll never survive.'

'I don't know why you both stay here,' said Agatha. 'I mean, what's in it for you?'

'I'm not leaving here until I find out who murdered Geraldine.' Agatha glanced quickly at Dawn Hammond. Dawn was studying her fingernails as if she had never seen anything so interesting before.

'You must have been very fond of her,' said Agatha.

'We were going to get married before Charlie Black came along.'

'I liked that film, *Rebecca*,' commented Dawn, looking up. 'Sometimes I feel I'm living in it.'

'Now, then, precious,' said Cyril, giving his wife an oily smile, 'you know I love only you.'

'So why can't we get the hell out of here?' demanded Dawn.

'I've told you and told you,' snapped Cyril, the smile disappearing. 'Her murderer is still at large.'

'It seems,' said Agatha, 'that Charlie Black did work for Brian McNally, who I gather might be some sort of drug baron. As a favour to Charlie, he kidnapped me trying to find out where the rest of the jewels were. Maybe he hired someone to sweat Geraldine and things got out of hand.'

James came into the dining room. 'Rain's easing up,' he said.

'Have you heard the news about that Deborah woman?' asked Cyril.

'No, what?'

'Went out at high tide and was swept out to sea.'

'This is horrible. I'll go round to the lifeboat station and see if there's any news.'

'Better wait until the tide goes down,' said Cyril.

'I'll go with you,' said Agatha. She realized in that moment how safe she had always felt with James at her side. Anything was better than sitting in this hotel wondering if someone was coming in to murder her.

The manager approached. 'The press are in the bar. I kept them in there until I knew you'd finished your breakfast.'

'I'll be off,' said James.

'You can't go until the tide goes down,' said Agatha, 'or you'll be the next casualty. Please wait for me. I won't be long.'

James seemed unaware of the Hammonds as he sat wrapped in misery. He could dimly hear Agatha regaling the press with stories of the brilliance of her detective agency. It was all his fault Deborah had come after him. He should never have phoned her.

At last Agatha came back carrying her coat. 'The rain's stopped,' she said. 'Where is the lifeboat station?'

'Along at West Point. I know where it is.'

Watery sunlight gilded the heaving grey waves as they walked along, followed by the press.

'What are they doing, coming after us?' asked James.

'I told them about Deborah. It took their minds right off my lack of success.'

'Sometimes you horrify me, Agatha.' James walked on in moody silence.

At last they reached the lifeboat station. The slip was empty. 'Still out looking for her,' said Agatha.

They all stood staring out to sea. Then one of the reporters who had been scanning the sea through his telescopic lens cried, 'The boat's coming back.'

They waited anxiously until they saw a little speck which grew gradually bigger and bigger. From behind them came the wail of a siren and then an ambulance drew up.

'She might be alive,' cried James. 'Please God she's still alive.'

The boat came nearer and nearer. 'There's a woman on board,' called the man with the lens. 'She's wrapped in blankets and drinking something.'

Much as she disliked Deborah, in that moment all Agatha could feel was admiration for any woman who could stay alive in such a sea.

The boat came ever closer. Now they could plainly see Deborah. An ambulance crew with a stretcher went down to meet the lifeboat.

Deborah was helped on to a stretcher while camera flashes went off all around.

As she was carried past James, she said, 'Darling, I was coming to meet you.'

Agatha winced.

She then joined the press, who were shouting questions at the lifeboat captain.

He held up his hands for silence and said, 'It

172

is incredible that she is alive. She is obviously a very powerful swimmer. How she managed to swim away from the sea wall and not get sucked into the undertow is beyond me. Then the current got hold of her and carried her along the coast. The waves were so high we nearly missed her.'

Agatha's one dismal thought was that she had no hope of competing with Deborah. First those legs and now a heroine.

James fell into step beside Agatha as they walked back to the hotel. 'It's not what you think,' he said.

'I was thinking of a large gin and tonic.'

'The thing is,' said James, 'I was supposed to have dinner with her and rushed down here at the last minute. So I phoned to apologize. She must have taken it as a come-on.'

'You didn't seem in any hurry to repulse her,' commented Agatha.

'How could I? She had come all this way. I'd better go to the hospital, I suppose.'

'Don't forget to take flowers. Oh, good, there's Patrick.'

Agatha chattered to Patrick on the road back. When they reached the hotel, James said, 'I would like a word in private with Agatha, Patrick.'

'Right,' said Patrick. 'I'm off to the police station.'

James turned to face Agatha, an apology hovering on his lips.

'Hey, there, you two,' called a cheerful voice. 'I've just arrived.'

Charles Fraith came strolling out of the hotel.

James's face darkened. He muttered, 'I'd better get to the hospital,' and strode inside.

'He was about to say something important to me,' raged Agatha when Charles joined her.

'If it was that important, he can say it later,' said Charles. 'I'd forgotten what a ghastly place this is. Let's walk somewhere civilized for a coffee and you can fill me in on all the details.'

In reception, James heard himself being hailed by the manager. 'Come into my office and have a glass of champagne,' called Mr Beeston.

'What's the celebration?' asked James, following him into the remains of what had once been a grand office with stained-glass windows and a magnificent mahogany desk.

'The bosses who own this place have told me they've had a terrific offer for this hotel.' He popped the cork on a bottle of champagne and poured two glasses.

'I can't think who would want it,' said James. 'It's about to be washed away any day now.'

'It's going to be one of the grandest casinos in England. They're going to build an enormous sea wall and have the entrance in Brighton Street.'

'Brighton Street?'

'The main street that runs parallel to the front.'

'I forgot the name of it. But there are shops there.'

'They're buying them out.'

'I'm surprised the residents didn't have something to say about it.'

'There's a meeting in the town hall tonight. The councillors and the mayor are all for it. It'll bring a lot of money into the town. I don't think the residents will object. The casino bosses have promised to raise the sea wall and extend it along the front.'

'It'll spoil the view.'

'Ever seen anyone in a casino looking *out*?'

'But the people who live along the seafront. A large wall would cut off the light from their houses.'

'They'll just have to realize it's the wall or their houses falling into the sea.'

'Who are these bosses?

'Regan Enterprises. An Irish firm, I believe. Drink up. Happy days.'

So James drank, his mind working furiously. What if there was criminal money behind all this, money that needed to be laundered somehow? Why should this Brian McNally, who appeared to be a major player in the criminal world, turn up simply to do an old lag a favour by sweating the whereabouts of some jewels out of Agatha? Perhaps he had bigger fish to fry in the area. It was a long shot, but he was determined to go to that meeting.

'At what time is the meeting tonight?' he asked.

'Seven o'clock.'

'Might take a look-in.'

'More champagne?'

'No, I'll leave you to it.'

James drove out to the hospital on the edge of town. He stopped at a florist's on the way and bought a bunch of flowers. He must be firm with Deborah and tell her that when she had recovered she should return to Carsely immediately.

Because she had become a local celebrity, Deborah had been put in a private room. To James's dismay, as he opened the door it was to find she was giving a press conference. He tried to back out, but Deborah saw him and called, 'Come in, darling.' Camera flashes went off in his face.

'Is there a romance here?' asked one reporter.

'Maybe,' said Deborah with a flutter of eyelashes.

'No,' said James firmly. 'I am here with my ex-wife to help her in a detective investigation. I'll leave you to it, Deborah.'

He made a hasty retreat. It was only when he was outside the room that he realized he was still clutching that bunch of flowers. He gave them to a passing nurse and asked her to deliver them to Mrs Fanshawe.

'I wish you hadn't come back,' Agatha was saying for what seemed to Charles like the umpteenth time.

'We've been over this and over this,' said

Charles, 'and you never give me the real reason. The real reason is that you're still besotted with James and you think I'm queering your pitch.'

'Well, he's twice been about to tell me something important and the last time you butted in. I mean, you take off when you feel like it, leaving me in the lurch, so why can't you just take off again?'

'Oh, all right. But not today. I'll set out tomorrow. You've never asked me to push off before. There's some villain around who thinks you know where some jewels are, and you still haven't found out who murdered Geraldine Jankers. I thought you'd be glad of the extra help.'

'I've got James and Patrick.'

'Aggie, I thought you had grown out of James.'

'I have! But I want to hear what it is he's going to say and he won't say it if you're still here!'

'In other words, I'm of use to you only when you feel like it?'

'That's how you've treated me.'

They glared at each other angrily. Then Charles began to laugh. 'Listen to us! You'd think we were lovers or something. Okay, Aggie, I'll be off tomorrow.'

Back at the hotel, James waylaid Agatha as she walked in. He looked excited. Charles went off to his room.

But James had no tender words to say or apology to make. He was full of what he had found out about the casino. Fighting down her disappointment, Agatha listened carefully. Then she

177

said, 'We'll both go tonight. By the way, Charles is leaving tomorrow.'

'Why is that? Oh, never mind. I can't wait to get to this meeting tonight.'

Up in his room, Charles switched on a small television set to watch the news. His interest sharpened as a picture of Deborah Fanshawe appeared on the screen. She was lying in a hospital bed looking very beautiful. Charles wondered how she had managed to find make-up to do her face or the lacy nightdress she was wearing when she had been taken straight to the hospital from the lifeboat.

A malicious smile curved his lips. He would get some flowers and go and see this beauty. That would irritate Agatha no end, and Charles felt like annoying her.

He went downstairs and asked for directions to the hospital. Betty, the receptionist, had just finished arranging flowers in a vase on the desk. Mr Beeston's voice sounded from the office, calling her in. Charles waited until she had left, picked up the vase full of flowers and went out of the hotel and round to the car park.

Deborah was beginning to get bored. She had slept a little after the press left and awoke feeling refreshed, but very annoyed with James Lacey. What on earth did he see in that charmless woman, Agatha?

The door opened and an expensively dressed

man entered carrying a vase of flowers. He had fair well-barbered hair and neat features.

'Hello,' he said. 'I'm Charles Fraith. I heard all about your adventure and thought I'd drop in and see you.'

'Fraith? Do you live at Barfield House?'

'Yes, that's me.'

Deborah gave him her best smile and said, 'Please sit down.'

Sir Charles Fraith, she thought. Was he married?

'What brings you down here?' she asked.

Charles set down the vase of flowers on a side table. There was very little water left in it, most of it having slopped on to the floor of his car.

'I'm a friend of Agatha Raisin.'

Deborah's face darkened.

'Anyway, she's fed up with me,' said Charles, 'so I might push off tomorrow. I say, you look great after all you've been through. Didn't know the hospital ran to such glamorous nighties.'

'The staff here are very kind. One nurse lent me make-up and another drove round to the hotel to pick up this nightdress and a few things from my room. All for the press conference, of course.'

'So why are *you* here?' asked Charles.

'I came to see James. He was running after me and I rather fancied him. But when I got here, he told me he wished I had never come.'

'He's like that, old James. Confirmed bachelor.'

'But he married that Raisin woman.'

'Didn't last, did it?'

179

'And what about you? Are you a confirmed bachelor?'

'Been married once. That was enough. Still, you never know when I might change my mind. Now, tell me about how you managed to survive.'

So Deborah told him, almost automatically, while her mind was calculating the advantages of being the next Lady Fraith. She would have a title. She would open fêtes and things.

When she had finished, Charles asked, 'When do you get out of here?'

'Tomorrow.'

'I could drive you home.'

'That's kind of you, but I don't want to leave my car down here.' Deborah hadn't quite given up on James Lacey. 'I may stay on for a few days until I completely recover. What about you?'

'I'll probably be around for a few days as well. We could have dinner or something, if you feel up to it.'

'That would be wonderful.'

Agatha left her room a mess of discarded clothes when she went to join James that evening. She had reluctantly rejected items like high heels, short skirts and blouses with plunging necklines for a warm sweater and trousers, walking shoes and coat.

James was elated and full of energy. Agatha wondered how she could prompt him into saying what he had been going to say.

The town hall was a red brick Victorian

monstrosity that not even John Betjeman could love. The hall was full.

Lined up on the platform and fronted by the mayor wearing his gold chain of office were several middle-aged and elderly men in dark suits. Agatha assumed they were the town councillors. To the left of the stage three men in very expensive suits and suntans were seated observing the proceedings. James pointed at them. 'I bet they're from Regan Enterprises,' he said.

The mayor began by making a speech about all the benefits the casino would bring to the town. Then he asked for questions. A woman rose to protest. She said they didn't want a casino. They had enough trouble with drugs without encouraging young people to get a gambling addiction. There was a roar of applause.

The mayor, a fat balding man with a pompous air, ridiculed her, saying that because of people like her, job opportunities would be lost and the town would never get that much-needed sea wall.

He answered each question in the same way until gradually the hall fell silent.

'Agatha!' said James suddenly.

But Agatha Raisin was on her feet marching towards the platform. She mounted the steps at the side and took the microphone from the startled mayor's hand.

'Are you all sheep?' she cried. 'Stand up to these bullies. Sea wall, indeed. What do you pay these tremendous council taxes for? There should be enough in the kitty to build one. Why

181

should pensioners starve to pay the damned council tax and then get this idea of a casino pushed on to them?'

There was a tremendous roar of applause. An elderly pensioner got to his feet and shouted above the noise, 'You sock it to them.'

'I think there should also be a full examination to make sure any money for this casino is clean. That is solely my opinion. Remember the case of the IRA man who was laundering money through buying property in Manchester?'

To James's alarm, he saw two burly security men hurrying towards the stage. He got to his feet.

'So I'll put it to a vote,' shouted Agatha. 'If you don't want this casino and think that the council should pay for a sea defence, raise your hands.'

A forest of hands went up.

The two security men rushed on to the platform, wrenched the microphone from Agatha's hand and began to drag her off the stage.

James confronted them. 'Leave her alone.'

'Get lost,' said one, releasing Agatha to swing a punch at James. James socked him on the jaw and he went down. Agatha belted the other one on the face with her capacious handbag.

'Let's get out of here,' she panted.

Carried on a wave of tumultuous cheers, they hurried from the hall with flashes from the cameras of the local press photographers going off in their faces.

'Run,' said James. 'We'll get my car and get out of this town for the rest of the evening.'

They arrived panting at the garage, got into James's car and drove off.

'You are a wretched woman,' said James with a laugh. 'But, by God, you were magnificent tonight. You've put yourself even more at risk than you ever were before. We'll need to think what to do with you.'

'I'm not running away,' said Agatha.

'We'll talk about it over dinner. We'll go to Brighton. By the time we get back, it should be quiet.'

'I should really have waited for the press,' said Agatha. 'It pays to advertise and I've got a business to run.'

'You've said it all. Let's just hope Regan Enterprises don't sue.'

'I said "in my opinion". They haven't a leg to stand on.'

'We'll see. But unless these casino people have the local police in their pockets, I think after what you said appears in the papers, they might feel obliged to look closely at Regan Enterprises.'

Over dinner in a pub, Agatha at last found the courage to ask, 'What was it you've been trying to say to me?'

James took a deep breath. 'I just wanted to say I was sorry I brought you to such a dreadful place for a holiday and I'm sorry I went off like that and left you.'

A broad smile lit Agatha's face. 'Apology accepted.'

He felt suddenly embarrassed. 'Do you think I could get a bowl of ice? My hand's throbbing dreadfully. In the movies, the hero socks everyone in sight and yet his hands don't seem to suffer.'

'Poor you,' said Agatha, feeling very wifely. She signalled to a waitress and ordered some ice. Then she tried to fight down the reanimation of her feelings for James. That way led to hurt. She had been enjoying her previous detachment from him.

She began to talk about Regan Enterprises. 'Do you know anyone in the City who could find out anything?'

'I've got a stockbroker friend. I could call him.'

The ice arrived. He wrapped some in a napkin and pressed it against his knuckles.

Then he suddenly smiled at Agatha.

'Well, here we are again,' he said.

Chapter Ten

'There's so much to find out,' said Agatha, taking out a small notebook. 'First: How much was Geraldine worth, and who inherits? Could be her dear old buddy Cyril. Second: Must check up on how Fred's businesses are doing. Third: Does Hammond have a criminal record? And fourth: Who's behind Regan Enterprises?'

'I'll phone my stockbroker friend in the morning and see if he can dig up anything on Regan Enterprises for me,' said James. 'You forgot a fifth thing.'

'What's that?'

'That mysterious flask of coffee in your room. Have the police found out if anything was in it? You have a right to ask the police for information on that.'

'Okay. I think I'll just ask Fred outright who inherits,' said Agatha. 'He's bound to know by now. I might phone Harry in the morning and ask him to check up on Fred's businesses. I want to give him as much to do as possible. He's so good. I wish he didn't have to go off to university.'

'Is Charles staying long?' asked James.

'I think he'll probably have left by the morning,' said Agatha.

Back at the hotel James escorted Agatha to her room and hesitated outside the door. Then he bent and kissed her on the cheek, and with a brief 'Goodnight' strolled along the corridor to his own room at the end.

'Men are impossible,' muttered Agatha. She put the large brass key in the lock, and then hesitated. She should have asked James to wait to make sure no one was lurking inside. She took a deep breath, unlocked the door and flung it open. She felt round it for the light switch and pressed it down. No light.

With a screech of alarm she ran along the corridor and hammered on James's door.

He jerked the door open and stared down into her frightened face. 'What's up?'

'The light won't come on in my room!'

'Come in. Don't go back. We'll call the police.'

Agatha sat on the edge of the bed shivering, listening to him call.

'They'll be along in a minute,' he said, replacing the phone.

But it was half an hour before a tired-looking Detective Sergeant Wilkins arrived flanked by two police officers.

They went along to Agatha's room. Agatha waited, trembling, in the corridor. Then Wilkins came back holding a spent light bulb.

'You need a new light bulb inside the door, that's all. The bedside lamps work.'

'Oh, I'm sorry to have dragged you out.'

'You're trouble, that's what you are,' said Wilkins. 'I heard all about the row at the town hall.'

'Someone has to stand up to people like that,' exclaimed Agatha.

'Okay, so why does it have to be you? I'm off.'

'Wait,' cried Agatha as he was walking away, following the two policemen.

'What is it now?'

'Who inherits Geraldine Jankers's money now that her son is dead?'

'Don't see any harm in you knowing. That friend of hers, Cyril Hammond.'

'Was it much?'

'A lot, believe you me. Now, if you want any more details, you'd better contact her solicitor.'

He turned away again.

'Wait!'

'Mrs Raisin, I'm tired. You drag me out on a silly errand and –'

'Does Cyril Hammond have a criminal record?'

He smiled. 'Now, that's the benefit of being in the force and not an amateur like you. Goodnight.'

'Pillock,' muttered Agatha. 'Sorry, James, I'd better get off to bed. But it was worth it to find out that Cyril inherits. He's a sleazy creep. I can imagine him luring her down to the beach.

187

I wonder if he has the rest of the jewels. I'd like a look at his room.'

'Agatha, he wouldn't carry them around with him.'

'But he might have given Dawn one piece. Wayne gave Chelsea that necklace.'

'Can we talk about this in the morning? I'm tired.'

'Okay. Goodnight.'

Agatha went along to her room. The door was still open. She went in and fumbled her way over to the bedside lamps and switched them on. She hurriedly undressed, washed and crawled into bed, but she left the lights burning.

Charles called at the hospital early the next morning to collect Deborah.

'Can you carry my bag, darling?' asked Deborah. 'It's just a few things of mine I got that nurse to collect for me from the hotel.'

'Right,' said Charles, although that 'darling' made him feel uneasy. But Deborah looked very attractive. She must be very strong and healthy, he thought, to come through that ordeal and look as though nothing had happened.

'Is that your car?' asked Deborah, as Charles led the way to a rather old and battered BMW.

'Yes, good old thing. Had it for years.'

'I can see that.' Need to make him get something more fitting when we're married, thought Deborah.

When they arrived at the hotel, it was to find

the reception crammed with reporters, photographers and television crews.

'Good heavens!' said Deborah. 'This all must be for me.' She raised her voice. 'Here I am!'

'Here she is!' cried a reporter. But no one was turning in Deborah's direction. They were all focusing on Agatha Raisin, who was descending the stairs.

Agatha faced a barrage of questions. Why had she hinted that laundered money might be used in the building of the casino? Did she know Regan Enterprises had withdrawn their offer? There was to be no casino in Snoth.

Back in Mircester, Detective Sergeant Bill Wong, Agatha's very first friend, watched the press conference with amusement. It was his day off. He knew of old that Agatha blundered around cases and then sometimes had brilliant flashes of intuition. That remark of hers about laundered money must have sent Regan Enterprises running for cover. If there was nothing in it, he was sure they would have gone ahead with their plans for the casino whatever the townspeople thought. A local television cameraman who had been at the town hall the night before had filmed Agatha making her speech. There were clips of it interposed throughout the press conference.

Then the smile left his face. Did Agatha know that if Regan Enterprises was a dicey operation and she had ruined their plans, they would be out for blood? Her blood.

Harry and Phil watched the same conference on a small television set in their office.

'You have to hand it to her,' said Phil. 'She's quite a lady.'

'She's a lady who is now in serious danger, if she wasn't before,' said Harry. 'Look, Phil, could we put a few of the minor cases on hold? I'm going down there. She'll need all the help she can get.'

Mrs Bloxby was enjoying a quiet cup of tea when the vicarage doorbell went. She sighed and got to her feet. That was the trouble with being a vicar's wife. The villagers felt free to call any time they felt like it.

She opened the door and looked at the neatly dressed businessman standing outside.

'Can I help you?'

'My name is John Belling,' he said, a smile crinkling his tanned face. 'I am thinking of buying somewhere in the village. Do you know if there's anything for sale?'

'There isn't anything at the moment,' said Mrs Bloxby. 'Or not that I know of. But sometimes people don't like estate agents' boards being put up. You could try some estate agents in Moreton-in-Marsh or Chipping Campden.'

190

'I heard an old friend of mine, Agatha Raisin, lives here.'

'You are unlucky. She is away at the moment.'

'What a pity. As a matter of fact, I was hoping to make a bid for her cottage.'

'Mrs Raisin has no intention of selling.'

'I am sure her cottage will be vacant very soon.'

'What makes you say that?'

'I'm psychic.' Again that smile.

Mrs Bloxby was suddenly afraid. 'You must excuse me,' she said hurriedly. 'I've left something on the stove.'

She shut the door and went quickly to the phone and telephoned Bill Wong. She breathlessly repeated the conversation she'd had with her visitor. 'Right,' said Bill when she'd finished. 'I'll be over with some men right away. I don't like the sound of this.'

Mrs Bloxby then phoned Agatha. Alarmed, Agatha asked for a description, and when Mrs Bloxby finished, she said, 'I think you've just had a visit from that drug baron, Brian McNally. Have you told the police?'

'Yes, Bill Wong is on his way over. Oh, do be careful, Agatha. Can't you and James go away for that holiday? Get out of the country?'

Agatha had taken the phone call at the reception desk. She went back to join James, who looked at her anxiously. She was trembling and her face was white. In a faltering voice she told him about

Mrs Bloxby's call. 'I'm running out of courage, James,' said Agatha and burst into tears.

She wanted him to take her in his arms and comfort her, but he handed her a large clean handkerchief and said, 'Let's go into the bar and talk about this. You need a stiff drink.'

Agatha gulped and blew her nose and went with him into the bar. 'This has become too dangerous,' said James. 'I think we should get away.'

Agatha dried her eyes and looked miserably at the smears of make-up on what had once been James's clean handkerchief.

'We can see Barret,' urged James. 'He'll be glad to see the back of us. We'll get in my car tomorrow and go over to France and tour around.'

'I feel such a wimp,' said Agatha. 'I'm terrified. Yes, we'll go.'

'Good girl. Let's see Barret.'

Barret looked relieved. He had received a call from the Mircester police, who were combing the area looking for Mrs Bloxby's mysterious caller.

'I forgot to phone Harry,' said Agatha. 'I meant to tell him to go to Lewisham and check on Fred's businesses. Then you've got to find out if your stockbroker friend can discover anything.'

'Agatha,' said James gently. 'None of that matters now. We're leaving.'

'So we are,' said Agatha dully. 'I forgot.'

It was not just the mysterious caller that had broken Agatha, it was the memory of that abduction. She felt she could not face any more adventures.

Said James, 'I'll get my car and we'll stay away from the hotel for the rest of the day. Then we'll come back this evening and pack. There's nothing here to keep us any longer.'

'We'll probably never know who killed Geraldine,' said Agatha.

'Does it matter? She was a pretty dreadful woman.'

Agatha walked silently beside him, but she felt it *did* matter. She had never run away from a case before.

Charles Fraith was feeling hunted. He, too, was out walking, but with Deborah, a Deborah who seemed to become more pushing and more pressing with every minute. The fact was that Deborah was still not quite recovered from her ordeal. She had bouts of shivering and a headache over her right temple. So she had thrown subtlety to the winds. She wanted to be Lady Fraith.

She had her arm through Charles's and was holding it in a strong grip. 'You know, darling,' she said, 'I think we'd make a great pair.'

Panicking slightly, Charles said, 'I don't know what Agatha would say to that.'

'What's she got to do with anything?'

'I more or less promised to marry her,' said Charles.

'What! She's running around with her ex!'

193

'That's nothing more than friendship. Agatha's quite capable of suing me for breach of promise.'

When they reached the hotel, Charles excused himself and said he had urgent phone calls to make and fled up to his room.

Deborah hesitated in reception. The whole thing was mad. She would confront Agatha Raisin and get it all sorted out. But she didn't want to do it in public.

She went up to the desk. 'Is Mrs Raisin in her room?'

'No. Out at the moment.'

'I thought so. I've some stuff she wanted me to leave in her room. Could you give me the key?'

Deborah was still regarded as a local heroine by the staff. Betty, the receptionist, handed over the key.

Deborah went upstairs and entered Agatha's room. She sat in a chair by the window, biting her lip, planning what she would say. The room was half dark from the mass of clouds covering the sky outside.

Downstairs, Betty looked up as a man in workman's overalls walked in carrying a tool bag.

'Got a call the carpet on the upstairs was coming loose,' he said.

'Go ahead,' said Betty indifferently, turning her eyes back to the magazine she had been reading.

The wind was blowing strongly and she felt irritated by the crash and thunder of the waves. Added to the noise was the barman next door playing Annie Lennox CDs at full volume.

The workman came back down.

'That didn't take long,' said Betty.

'Small job,' he said. 'See ya.'

Betty returned to reading an article about Prince William.

She became aware of someone standing in front of her and, with a sigh, looked up again.

'Is Mrs Raisin in?' asked Patrick.

'No, she's out,' said Betty, tearing herself out of a fantasy of seeing Prince William walk into the hotel. 'But Mrs Fanshawe is waiting for her in her room.'

'Why? Why did you give her the key?'

'Because she said she had some stuff of Mrs Raisin's to leave in her room.'

'You shouldn't have given her key to anyone. I'll go and get it back.'

Patrick mounted the stairs and went along to Agatha's room. The door was not locked. He opened it and went in.

He let out an exclamation of horror. There was blood spattered on the walls and a figure slumped in a chair with half its head blown away.

James and Agatha were driving towards Brighton. Agatha could feel a lifting of her spirits. They would escape tomorrow and she need never see Snoth-on-Sea or that terrible hotel again.

Her mobile phone rang. 'Don't answer that,' said James.

'I must tell Patrick that I'm leaving,' said Agatha. 'It may be him.'

It was Patrick, a Patrick unusually flustered and shaken.

'Better get back here,' he said. 'Deborah Fanshawe has been shot. She was waiting in your room and some hitman must have thought it was you.'

'We'll be with you as soon as possible.'

Agatha switched off her mobile. 'Turn the car, James,' she said wearily. 'Something truly awful has happened.'

Chaos in front of the hotel – police, photographers, reporters and television crew. For once in her life, ducking her head and avoiding the questions shouted at her, Agatha let James hurry her into the hotel.

A policewoman approached them. 'Mrs Raisin?'

'Yes.'

'You are to go into the bar. You will be interviewed there.'

They went into the bar. Charles was there looking white and strained. At another table sat Cyril and his wife, Dawn.

James and Agatha sat down with Charles. 'What really happened?' asked James.

Charles looked more shaken than Agatha had ever seen him look before.

'It's all my fault,' he said. 'She was so pushy and she was practically on the verge of proposing to me, so I said I was promised to Aggie.'

'You what?' Agatha stared at him.

'I just wanted to get her off my back. She must have got the key to your room and decided to confront you, and some villain thought it was you and blasted her head off with a shotgun.'

'How do you know it was a shotgun?' asked James.

'Patrick said half her head was missing and there was blood and brains spattered all over the walls.'

'Can't we get a drink?' demanded James, looking at Agatha's white face. 'Oh, here's Patrick.'

Patrick, looking more lugubrious than usual, slumped down in a chair opposite them.

'What exactly happened?' asked James.

'It seems Mrs Fanshawe got the key from Betty saying she had some stuff of Agatha's to leave in her room. After Mrs Fanshawe had gone upstairs, a man in worker's overalls and carrying a tool bag came in and said he was to repair part of the stair carpet. She told him to go ahead. After a short time he came back down and walked out of the hotel.'

'It wasn't Brian McNally in person,' said Agatha shakily, 'because he was in Carsely putting the wind up Mrs Bloxby by saying he wanted to buy my cottage. I know it must have been him from her description.'

'There's something else,' said Patrick. 'My contact told me that Regan Enterprises is no more. Their offices in Dublin burned down last night and the directors have disappeared.'

'So I was right,' said Agatha. 'It must have been dodgy money.'

'I'm going to get us all some drinks,' said James.

'I'll come with you,' said Charles. 'Why don't we just take a bottle of brandy and some glasses?'

They had just come back from the bar with a bottle and glasses when Superintendent Willerby walked in with Wilkins and Barret and a policewoman.

'We'll take you one by one,' said the superintendent. 'Starting with you, Mrs Raisin. Where were you when Mrs Fanshawe was in your room? That would be, according to the receptionist, at three p.m.'

'I was with James, Mr Lacey, driving to Brighton when I got a call from Patrick Mulligan telling me what happened.'

'What was she doing in your room? She told the receptionist that you had asked her to leave some things in your room.'

'I never told her any such thing.' Agatha's beady eyes turned on Charles. 'I think Sir Charles Fraith might have an answer to your questions.'

'Sir Charles?'

Charles shifted awkwardly in his chair. Despite her shock and distress, Agatha could not help feeling pleased to see the usually unflappable Charles looking uneasy.

'It was like this,' he said. 'Deborah, Mrs Fanshawe, was pursuing me. She was almost on the point, I felt, of proposing marriage. I panicked and told her I was promised to Aggie.'

'Meaning Mrs Raisin.'

'Yes.'

'Go on.'

'She was a very pushy woman and I feel she was waiting for Agatha to have it out with her.'

'The light in that room is very dim. She was looking out of the window,' said Willerby. 'I am afraid we have to assume that the murderer mistook her for Mrs Raisin.'

Patrick said, 'Do you think Brian McNally sent a hit man after Agatha? He wouldn't know exactly what Agatha looked like.'

'It's a possibility. Now I will take each of you in turn . . .'

'Thank goodness that's over,' said Agatha after what seemed like hours of questioning.

'There's one bad thing about it,' said James. 'We can't leave.'

Charles said, 'Do you mean you two were thinking of leaving? That's not like you, Aggie.'

'Oh, shut up!' said James furiously. 'You should be worried about yourself. Willerby doesn't quite buy the hitman suggestion, which leaves you number one suspect.'

'Sorry to disappoint you. They've searched my room and haven't found any weapon.'

'It's all your fault,' said Agatha bitterly. 'What were you doing chasing after Deborah anyway?'

'She was, at first glance, a very attractive woman.'

They were still sitting in the bar. Agatha looked across the room in surprise as Harry walked in.

'What are you doing here?' asked Agatha.

'I thought you could do with some more protection,' said Harry, joining them. 'What's going on? The hotel is crawling with police. Some ferocious-looking woman even demanded a DNA sample. I nearly gagged when she shoved that stick in my mouth. Then I had to produce identification and all that.'

Agatha told him about Deborah's murder. Harry listened carefully and then said, 'You should change your room again.'

'The police have done that for me,' said Agatha. 'Their forensic people are working on my old room. Patrick, I keep forgetting to ask you. Did you find out if the police discovered anything in that flask of coffee?'

'Nothing in it, or the milk, sugar or biscuits. She may have had orders to kill you and took along that tray to look like room service. She says she was supposed to wait for you and give you a warning, but she chickened out.'

'I'm getting out of this place as soon as I can,' said Charles. 'I know the chief constable. I mean, if I leave my address, it should be enough.'

James's blue eyes glinted. 'You mean you're not going to stay around to help us guard Agatha?'

'Lots of you here,' said Charles callously. 'I'm starving. Hey, wait a bit! You know who was missing when we were all in the bar? Fred Jankers.'

'I asked about that,' said Patrick. 'He'd gone home to Lewisham to bury Wayne and Chelsea. He's due back tomorrow.'

'I wonder why on earth he's coming back

here,' said Agatha. 'Anyway, Cyril Hammond is my number one suspect. He inherits Geraldine's money.'

'Why is he still here?' asked Harry.

'He says he wants to wait until the murderer of his precious Geraldine is found.'

'Hard to believe,' said James.

Agatha looked at him. 'He was devoted to Geraldine. Isn't it odd? I mean, she was a frumpy loud-mouthed woman and yet she could get men devoted to her.'

'Sounds like you, Aggie,' said Charles cheerfully. 'I'm off to get something to eat.'

'You're forgetting something,' said Agatha. 'Police cars will be arriving shortly to take us to Lewes to make our official statements.'

'Then I'd better eat fast,' said Charles. 'I'll go to the kitchen and see if they have any sandwiches.'

'Why don't you bring in a large plate of them,' shouted Agatha to his retreating back.

Just when they began to think he had forgotten about them, Charles appeared, following a waitress who was bearing a huge plate of sandwiches.

'I should have asked for coffee,' said Charles, 'but I don't think we've got time now.'

'I'm a bit tiddly,' mourned Agatha.

James arranged sandwiches for her on a plate. 'Here, eat some of these. Good blotting paper.'

Agatha did her best, but each mouthful seemed to stick in her throat.

At last they were summoned to the cars. 'You don't need to go,' said Agatha to Harry. 'Could you get to Lewisham and see what you can find out about Fred Jankers's businesses?'

'Will do,' said Harry.

They all, with the exception of Harry, exited the hotel and fought their way to the police cars through the shouts of the press and camera flashes.

The whole business of questioning took longer than anyone could have expected. It went on for the rest of the day and then they were put up in a hotel for the night and the grilling resumed the next day.

Agatha found that this time she was being asked questions by the Special Branch. Why had she assumed that the money might be laundered? On and on it went, until she seemed to hear her tired voice echoing in her brain.

And then, all at once, they were free to go. The policeman who was driving Agatha, James and Charles said as they got out of the car, 'There's a storm warning. Going to hit here the day after tomorrow.'

They all ate a later meal in the dining room, not talking much, not one of them feeling they wanted to talk much any more.

Agatha had drunk a lot of wine at dinner and she staggered as James escorted her to her hotel room door.

'Alcohol isn't the solution, Agatha,' said James.

'Oh, pish off,' said Agatha wearily.

She went into her room, locked the door

behind her and put a chair under the door handle. She sat down on the bed and took off her shoes. Then she felt too weary to undress. She slumped back on the bed and hung on to it as it seemed to revolve round the room. Her eyes closed and she plunged into a drunken sleep.

In the morning she awoke with a dry mouth and a blinding headache. She was still dressed and felt as if alcohol had seeped out of her pores and into her clothes.

Agatha forced herself to strip and take a shower. But by the time she emerged from the bathroom, she felt too ill to dress. The phone rang. It was James.

'How are you?' he asked.

'I feel ill,' moaned Agatha. 'I'm going back to bed.'

'I told you that alcohol was not the solution. I —'

Agatha replaced the receiver. She swallowed two painkillers and went back to bed.

Betty Teller turned over the reception desk to Nick Loncar and made her way out of the hotel, looking uneasily at the heaving sea. There had been storm forecasts on the radio all day, the radio she kept under the desk tuned to a pop-music programme. The announcer had even interrupted a fab Robbie Williams record to warn about the approaching storm.

She turned off the seafront into the shelter of a side street and bumped into a handsome young man.

'I'm sorry,' he said. 'Didn't look where I was going. But if I've got to bump into someone, I'm lucky it was a pretty girl like you.'

Betty looked at him, her mouth hanging a little open. He was *gorgeous*.

'Can I make it up to you? Buy you a drink?'

Betty did not hesitate for a moment. 'That would be nice.'

He had curly dark hair and an olive skin. His clothes were casual but expensive. They went together into the Green Man. No pole dancers were performing and the bar was nearly empty.

He bought her a Bacardi Breezer and fetched a half-pint of lager for himself. They sat at a table.

'Now what does a pretty girl like you do for a living?'

'I'm a receptionist at the murder hotel.'

'You mean the Palace?'

'Yes.'

'It's a wonder you don't leave.'

'I can't let the manager down,' said Betty virtuously. The real reason she stayed on was because of the press. Betty had dreams of being 'discovered' and becoming a television star.

'I read about it in the papers,' he said. 'That Mrs Raisin must be one tough bird.'

'I think she's feeling the strain,' said Betty. 'It's not only the murders. There's that ex-husband of hers, Mr Lacey. I don't know what's going on there except she's still mad about him. You can see it in her face. I'd guess he divorced her and she wants him back.'

'Doesn't he sleep with her?'

'Nope. Separate rooms.'

He had a slight foreign accent. Betty wished one of her friends would come in and see her with this handsome man. And he was so interested in everything she said. He got her to describe everyone in the hotel and what they were like.

After her third drink, Betty realized she would have to go to the loo. She excused herself.

But when she returned to the bar with her make-up carefully repaired, there was no sign of the young man.

She asked the barman where he had gone, hoping he had gone to the loo as well, but he said her escort had walked out as soon as she left the bar.

Betty felt wretched. She didn't even know his name.

Agatha joined James for dinner. She was in a foul mood. Her hip had started hurting again. She knew it was arthritic but had gone in for a course of Pilates exercises and the pain had receded. But now it was back again. She felt old, slightly sick and in pain.

James, on the other hand, was buoyant and energetic.

'I've been thinking,' he said, 'that they won't

keep us here much longer and then we can be off. We could go to Paris first and then motor down to the south.'

Agatha looked at him in silence. The wind screamed and howled outside like a banshee.

She thought of her cottage in Carsely and her beloved cats. She thought of the strain of being in James's company, sleeping in separate rooms, waiting for the love that never came.

At last she looked across the table at him and said, 'I want to go home.'

'But some sunshine would do us the world of good.'

'I do really want to go home, James.'

'You're tired and upset and you've probably got some of that hangover left. I hope you're not taking to the bottle.'

Agatha felt a stabbing pain at her hip. She got up stiffly. 'Don't lecture me. I'm going back to bed.'

'Do that. You'll feel better in the morning.'

Chapter Eleven

Agatha felt she simply had to get out of the hotel the next morning. Despite the warnings of an approaching storm, the day was sunny and blustery. She asked Patrick to accompany her, not wanting to see either Charles or James. Patrick hardly ever spoke unless spoken to.

Patrick quietly accepted Agatha's explanation that she needed some exercise and that the hotel was beginning to feel like a prison.

As they walked along and round the streets, she could almost see the quiet fishing village as it must have been in James's youth. In fact, apart from the widened main street, the centre of Snoth was quite small, with housing estates on the outskirts. The houses in the narrow streets leading up from the seafront to the main street looked as if they had once probably been fishermen's cottages. It was the large chain stores in the main street and the seedy little shops in the side streets which, she guessed, had robbed the town of its charm and innocence. It was almost as if the town had turned to catering for the unemployed with amusement arcades and sex shops. White-faced, seedy-looking youth hung out at the street corners.

'I'm feeling better now,' said Agatha at last. 'Let's have a coffee.'

She checked one café after another, peering in the windows to find out if there were welcoming ashtrays on the tables.

At last she found one. It advertised snacks and light refreshments. It was not very cosy, having Formica tables and very hard chairs, but each table had little tin ashtrays of the type the proprietor didn't mind having stolen.

Agatha and Patrick ordered coffees and Agatha lit a cigarette and then watched the blue smoke drifting in a sunbeam shining through the plate-glass window.

Sunbeams were the enemy of smokers, thought Agatha, highlighting just how much of the poisonous stuff you were sending out into the surrounding air.

'I can't help thinking about Deborah,' she said. 'I didn't like the woman, but she was so very brave to have survived that sea. What am I going to do, Patrick? James wants me to go off on holiday with him, but I only want to go home.'

Said Patrick, 'The best thing then would be to persuade James to go home for a couple of weeks to see everything is all right.'

'That might be a good idea. I should really get back to the office. Poor Phil must be sadly overworked.'

'I spoke to him last night. He said to send Harry back as soon as possible. He says he can manage all right with Harry, but he finds it tough being on his own. Of course, he's in his seventies.'

'I hate the idea of getting old,' said Agatha. She shifted in her chair. No nasty twinges this morning. 'How do you fancy Cyril Hammond for the murder of Geraldine? He seems to have been devoted to her, but that could all be an act.'

'He's certainly one person who might have persuaded her to leave the hotel. My contact at the station is trying to find out if he has any sort of criminal record. If you get permission to leave, will you really go and leave the murder of Geraldine unsolved?'

'I don't know. I would like to go home, but at least here there are a lot of police around. Brian McNally has been seen in Carsely. I would be an easier target there.'

'In that case, perhaps James's idea is sound – get out of the country and disappear for a bit.'

'The trouble is, I don't really know what James thinks of me. I thought when he suggested a holiday together that perhaps he might want to marry me again. But when I was married to him before, it wasn't comfortable. It was like being a houseguest rather than a wife. He found fault with everything I did. So why should he want to get back together with me?'

'Perhaps he's thinking of approaching old age and doesn't want to be alone. Men always like to think there'll be some woman there to look after them in their dotage.'

'Hardly a romantic picture,' said Agatha drily. 'What do you plan to do today?'

'Hang around the police station and see what I can pick up.'

'I need a break from it all,' said Agatha. 'I'll drive off somewhere and spend the day alone.'

'Is that wise? McNally or one of his villains could still be looking for you.'

'But I'll feel like a sitting duck if I stay in the hotel. Phone me if you find out anything.'

Agatha drove out of the underground car park experiencing a feeling of freedom. She drove up over the downs and then cruised through small villages. She stopped for lunch at a pub and then returned to her car, still reluctant to go back to the hotel.

She went down into Brighton, parked the car, and walked to the Pavilion, that famous folly of the Prince Regent. She walked around the rooms, wearying at last of so much garishness and so much gold leaf.

Then Agatha spotted a second-hand bookshop in the Lanes, bought herself a chick-lit book, found a café and settled down to read.

It was the usual mixture – the good girlfriend, the gay friend, the handsome friend whom the heroine had always regarded as a brother and the usual catalogue of Versace dresses and Jimmy Choo shoes.

But it was undemanding reading and she enjoyed it. When she finally left the café, the sky was becoming black overhead and the seagulls, wheeling and screaming, looked startlingly white against the inky backdrop.

A classic cinema was advertising *Monsieur Hulot's Holiday*. Agatha remembered someone telling her it was very funny. She bought a ticket and went in, buying herself a tub of popcorn and a Coke at the little shop in the foyer.

There were very few customers in the cinema. Agatha settled down in the dark and prepared to enjoy herself.

She found the film very funny indeed, and laughing at Jacques Tati's antics enabled her to forget about murder.

When she emerged after the film, the wind was blowing in great violent gusts.

Back in the shelter of her car, she still did not feel like returning to Snoth and decided to have dinner in the pub where she had had lunch earlier. She ate a generous helping of roast duck and followed it up with an equally generous helping of sticky toffee pudding covered in double cream.

The waistband of her skirt was uncomfortably tight when she left, but she felt soothed and relaxed.

Gusts of wind buffeted the car as she drove back towards Snoth-on-Sea. When she parked the car and emerged from the underground car park, she could only be glad it was not yet high tide. Already the roar of the waves was deafening.

A pile of sandbags blocked the hotel entrance and she had to climb over them. As she collected

211

her key, Nick Loncar handed her a note. It was from James, typewritten as usual, thought Agatha, as if he considered the written word too intimate.

It read: 'Patrick tells me you went off for a drive. Meet me for breakfast at nine o'clock. There is something we need to discuss. James.'

Agatha crumpled it up in disgust. No 'Love, James' or 'Affectionately yours, James.'

'Bad news?'

Agatha turned and saw Charles standing there. 'Where have you been?' he asked.

'Got fed up with the hotel and went off by myself for the day. Why are you still here? Didn't you get permission to leave?'

'I can go tomorrow. Let's have a talk, Aggie. I'm worried about you.'

'Can't I just go to bed? I'm tired.'

'Just one drink in the bar.'

'All right. Just the one.'

Charles ordered a whisky for himself and a gin and tonic for Agatha.

'So what's all this about?' asked Agatha.

'It's about you and James.'

'What about it?'

'I was talking to James today. He seems confident that you and he will take this holiday together.'

'I'm not confident we will. I just want to get home.'

'I feel somehow sure that James will persuade you at the last minute. Although I behave like a callous rat sometimes, I am your friend. Have you ever seriously considered that the attraction

212

James holds for you is because he is nearly always unavailable in some way? You go on like a battered wife, always returning for another helping of abuse. Maybe you need some form of therapy.'

'There is nothing up with me,' retorted Agatha. 'As a matter of fact, I am going to go home as soon as I can.'

'We'll see. Just don't go back and after a few weeks start mourning what you might see as a lost opportunity.'

'Charles, I am sure all this lecturing is well meant, but I am tired. That shrieking storm is getting on my nerves.'

'I hope the hotel lasts the night,' said Charles. 'But think about what I said.'

At one in the morning, Nick Loncar looked up from the football magazine he was reading and saw a man standing in front of him. Nick could hear the waves thundering over the sea wall and wondered how this man had managed to keep dry.

'Do you want a room, sir?' he asked.

The man smiled. He had a pleasant, tanned face and he was expensively dressed. 'I am from Lewes CID,' he said. 'I am afraid I'll need to have another word with Mrs Raisin. Something's just happened.'

'May I see some ID?' asked Nick cautiously.

He flashed a card at him.

'We'll use the bar,' said the man. 'What we have to discuss is top secret, so I want you to put on the lights in the bar and make yourself scarce.'

'Will do.' Nick hesitated. 'How did you manage to get in here without getting wet?'

The man's eyes narrowed. 'You are impeding the police in an investigation,' he said in a voice heavy with menace.

'All right, all right,' said Nick. 'I'll call her.'

He rang from the desk and spoke to Agatha. When he put down the phone he said, 'Mrs Raisin says to give her ten minutes to get dressed.'

'Right. Just put on a couple of lights in the bar and get lost.'

'I'll be in the manager's office if you want me.'

Agatha walked down into the reception area and was immediately deafened by the roar of the storm. The wind howled and great waves crashed against the door of the hotel.

She went into the bar. Only two lamps were lit. She saw a man sitting over by the long windows, his back to her.

She approached. 'You asked to see me?'

Nick sat at the manager's desk, biting his thumb nervously and eyeing the phone. He had received a rocket from the police after the murder of Geraldine because he had said he had not noticed anyone leaving the hotel around the time she was murdered. The fact was, he had gone into the bar and stretched out in one of the armchairs for a sleep. Nick also worked during the day at a pub in Snoth as barman.

He made up his mind. He phoned Lewes police headquarters and asked them if they had sent a detective to interview Mrs Raisin.

The man in the bar rose as he heard Agatha approach. He turned and smiled. 'Sit down, Mrs Raisin.'

Agatha let out a gasp of fear. 'Brian McNally,' she said.

He was holding a gun on her. How odd the workings of the frightened mind, thought Agatha. I don't know if that's a pistol or a revolver. I'm the pre-gun generation. I can't tell one from the other.

'Sit down,' he ordered again.

Agatha sat down, her heart as tumultuous as the raging storm outside.

He raised his voice against the storm. 'You are one nosy interfering bitch and it's going to be a pleasure to get rid of you. This casino deal was going to be sweet as a nut. You've ruined my business.'

Goodbye, everybody, thought Agatha. She suddenly felt calm. She didn't know if there was a God, but Mrs Bloxby believed in one, so she asked Mrs Bloxby's God either to let her die with dignity or to save her.

He levelled the gun and pointed it at her heart.

'Not going to beg for your life? I'd like that.'

'Fry in hell, you bastard,' said Agatha.

At that moment a huge wave crashed against the long windows of the bar, shattering them. As the sea poured in, Brian half turned his head in alarm. A flying shard of glass embedded itself in his neck. Agatha threw herself on the floor and then felt herself being swept up in a tide of seawater towards the bar. As the undertow began to drag her back, she clutched on to the foot rail of the bar.

Then, as the water receded, she stumbled to her feet and ran screaming and splashing through the now flooded reception. Still screaming, she ran up the stairs and pounded on James's door.

James answered it. Agatha shot past him, babbling, 'Brian McNally was in the bar. He tried to shoot me.'

'Sit down,' ordered James. 'I'll call the police.'

The police arrived very quickly, alerted by Nick's call. Not being able to approach the front of the hotel, they had climbed over the garden wall at the side and had come in through an open fire door.

Agatha had had time to change into dry clothes, which James had fetched from her room.

Sergeant Wilkins was the first to appear. 'Tell us what happened, Mrs Raisin.'

In a shaky voice Agatha told him all she knew.

'Brian McNally's dead,' said Wilkins. 'A piece of glass from the shattered windows sliced an artery in his neck. He bled to death. He was nearly swept out to sea. We found his body jammed under a sofa next to the windows. Evidently he got Nick Loncar to get you down to the bar by saying he was a detective and flashing a fake ID. Loncar phoned the police. The police found a fire door open and we assume he got in that way. We got here as soon as we could. It's a mess out there. The fire brigade and ambulance men will be searching the houses on the seafront in the hope that the residents have survived the storm. You'll need to come along to the police station and make an official statement.'

'Can't you see she's still in shock?' demanded James angrily. 'I'll bring her along in the morning.'

'Very well. We'll send someone for her at seven o'clock.'

'Make it nine,' said James. 'Let her get some sleep.'

Agatha, who in her fantasies about James had imagined being rescued by him and spending the night in his arms, now only wanted to get to the privacy of her own room and have a good cry.

She assured James she would be all right and locked her door. She found she was shivering and stripped off and had a hot shower. She changed into her nightdress and crawled into bed and fell into a sleep tortured with dreams of being lost at sea and fighting up one wave and down the next and never having land in sight.

She awoke early. Sun was streaming in the window. She got out of bed and looked out to see if the sea had receded, forgetting that her room overlooked a weedy garden at the back of the hotel.

Agatha got dressed and went down to the dining room to find it full of shattered glass and upturned tables and chairs. Charles appeared behind her.

'What a night,' he said.

'Haven't you heard what happened?'

'No.'

Agatha told him. 'Let's go up to my room,' said Charles. 'My feet are getting wet. The carpets are sodden.'

Wearing a pair of bright pink Wellington boots, Betty came into the hotel.

'Oh, Mrs Raisin, the police stopped me outside and told me what had happened. The hotel's finished. I'll need to look for another job. There was something odd I should have told you about. I got talking to a young man and he took me for a drink. He asked me all sorts of questions about you and Mr Lacey and when I went to the loo and came back, he'd disappeared.'

'You'd better tell the police,' said Agatha.

Upstairs in Charles's room, Agatha said, 'I wonder why that young man was asking questions about me.'

'Probably one of McNally's boys trying to find out for him what they could,' said Charles. 'Before he thought up the detective idea, he maybe planned to try something like sending up a note pretending it came from James. You haven't any make-up on.'

'So what?'

'So you'd feel better if you put a bit of paint on. You're awfully white. The press will be there and you don't want to look like a ghost. Cheer up. You know what I think? I think with McNally dead, that will be the end of attempts on your life. The head of the serpent has been chopped off. You've the devil's own luck, Agatha.'

'Or maybe it was Mrs Bloxby's God.'

'What are you talking about?'

'Never mind.'

The police came and took Agatha to the police station along with Nick and Betty. They had to walk because the seafront was a shattered mess of fallen slates, bricks, broken glass and flotsam and jetsam.

Agatha was glad she had made up her face because it seemed as if all the world's press were outside the police station.

Agatha, Nick and Betty were taken off to separate interviewing rooms.

Faced by Barret and Wilkins, Agatha wearily told her story all over again. And again and again.

At last Barret said, 'Well, that wraps it up. I must say we're pretty happy. One highly dangerous villain dead. And a money-laundering operation broken for the moment. McNally was the kingpin, and with him out of the way I don't think you should have anything to fear any longer, Mrs Raisin. I think you should go home.'

'What about the death of Geraldine Jankers?'

'We've come to the conclusion it had something to do with that jewel theft. If McNally could hire killers to attack you, then he would not have blinked at getting rid of Geraldine to do Charlie Black a favour.'

'But what if it had nothing to do with McNally?'

'Case closed. Go home, Mrs Raisin.'

Agatha emerged from the interview room to find Charles waiting for her. 'I thought you could do with some breakfast before we all start filling in insurance forms.'

'What for?'

'All the cars in the car park are a wreck, including your rented car.' He turned to the desk sergeant. 'Is there a back way out of this station?'

'I'll show you the way.'

'Unless, Aggie, you want to face the press.'

'Not now,' said Agatha.

Agatha was comforted and sustained by a large breakfast of sausage, eggs, bacon, beans and fried bread, washed down with mugs of black coffee.

What was even more surprising was that Charles paid for it.

'I'd better phone the car rental company as soon as I get back,' said Agatha. 'I want to go home today.'

'Why bother? I phoned my insurance company early this morning and I've got a courtesy car waiting for me at a garage outside the town. I'll run you back to Carsely. I'll order a taxi to wait for us round the corner from the hotel and we'll need to lug our bags round to it. It'll be a while before anything can drive up to the front.'

Agatha had hoped to escape the press, but the storm damage was also news and television crews were filling the seafront. For once in her life all she said was a gruff 'No comment.'

She arranged to meet Charles downstairs in an hour's time. Duckboards had been placed across the wet carpet in the hall.

In her room, Agatha phoned Patrick and told him she was leaving and that she would settle his bill as well as her own. Then she phoned the car rental company and told them what had happened, saying that she would fill in the accident forms and send them off.

The phone rang almost as soon as she replaced the receiver. It was Mrs Bloxby. 'I've just heard the news on the radio,' said the vicar's wife. 'Would you like me to drive down there?'

'It's all right, Mrs Bloxby. I'm coming home.'

'I'll see Doris Simpson and give her a casserole to put in your kitchen. I won't talk any more because you must be feeling shaken. Ring me when you get home.'

Agatha packed quickly, looking sadly at all the flimsy holiday garments that she had hoped to wear. She had just finished when Charles knocked at the door.

'Taxi's waiting.'

Charles took hold of Agatha's case, and they had just reached the top of the stairs when James came to join them.

'Where on earth have you been, Agatha?' he demanded.

'At the police station. I've got to go, James.'

'Agatha, I thought we were going on holiday together.'

'I'm going home,' said Agatha. 'Besides, your car's a wreck.'

'What?'

'Didn't you know? The car park was flooded and all the cars are wrecked.'

'Look, wait at the hotel until I get a replacement. It should only take a few days. You can stay at the hotel with me until then.'

'Taxi's waiting,' muttered Charles.

'I can't wait a minute longer in this arsehole of the world,' said Agatha. 'I'm off.'

'Agatha, I'm warning you. This is your last chance.'

'Just who the hell do you think you are? Come on, Charles.'

The taxi dropped them off at the garage and Charles signed the papers for a courtesy car – a new Peugeot.

They drove out of Snoth and Agatha heaved a sigh of relief as she watched the housing estates on the outskirts of the town pass by and recede into the distance.

'Feeling all right about James?' asked Charles.

'I don't feel anything other than relief at getting away from that place.'

Agatha's mobile phone rang. 'Aren't you going to answer that?' asked Charles.

'No, I'm going to switch the damned thing off!'

Agatha felt her spirits rise as the miles between her and Snoth-on-Sea increased. Going home! She had never felt so passionately about it before. And when Charles finally turned down the road leading to Carsely, where the trees arched on either side to form a green tunnel, she felt like a hunted animal returning to its burrow.

'I won't wait,' said Charles, carrying her suitcase up to the door. 'I'll call you.'

Agatha entered her cottage and cried a welcome to her cats. They looked up at her with indifference, a sort of cat's way of punishing her for her absence. Dumping her suitcase in the hall, she went through to the kitchen. The promised casserole from Mrs Bloxby was on the kitchen table. 'Lamb stew,' said a neat little label on the top.

The doorbell rang, making her jump nervously. She went through to the front door and peered through the spyhole. Bill Wong stood outside. She flung open the door with a cry of welcome.

'Come in, Bill.'

'Mrs Bloxby phoned me to say you were coming back.'

Agatha's cats, Hodge and Boswell, ran to Bill, mewing and purring a welcome.

'You've been having adventures,' said Bill, following her through to the kitchen.

'I'm glad it's all over. Coffee? Oh dear, I haven't any milk.' Agatha opened the fridge. 'Yes, I have. God bless Mrs Bloxby.'

'I'll have a cup. So it's all over, is it?'

'The police down there have come to the conclusion that one of Brian McNally's hitmen killed Mrs Jankers.'

'Why?'

Agatha plugged in the kettle. 'Well, because of the jewels from that robbery. He must have demanded them, she said she hadn't got them, and got killed.'

Bill said, 'Somehow, the timing's out. Charlie Black at that time was out of prison, even if he had an alibi, so it stands to reason that McNally wouldn't step in until after Charlie got arrested.'

'The police down there are happy,' said Agatha mulishly. 'What a long time this kettle's taking to boil.'

'You've only just plugged it in. You must have had several bad frights.'

'Yes, I did. But I find it's not healthy to brood on them.'

'Not healthy to block everything out of your mind either.'

The kettle boiled. Agatha put instant coffee in two mugs, filled them with hot water, carried them to the table and then lifted the milk out of the fridge.

'What are you trying to say?' asked Agatha. 'Do sit down and help yourself to milk.'

Bill pulled a chair up to the table and sat down. Hodge climbed up on him and hung round his shoulders like a fur stole and Boswell lay on his lap.

'I'm saying that I think Geraldine Jankers might have been murdered by someone in that hotel. Just a feeling I've got.'

'You weren't there. I think the police have got it right this time.'

'Where's James?'

'Still there, as far as I know.'

'I thought you would come back with him.'

'Well, I didn't,' snapped Agatha. 'How's your coffee?'

'Okay.'

'And how's your love life?'

'Dormant. Tell you what, run through the Jankers case again for me.'

'Bill, I'm tired. I don't want to think about it any more.'

'Then I'll be on my way.' Bill gently lifted

down her cats and stood up. 'There's just one interesting thing you might not know.'

'What's that?' Agatha followed him as he walked to the door.

'Cyril Hammond has a record.'

'Of what?'

'As a young man he assaulted a woman in a pub. Mind you, both of them were drunk, but he half strangled her before the customers could pull him off. Charged with actual bodily harm and sent to the cooler for eighteen months. Goodbye, Agatha.'

Bill walked out of the front door and closed it gently behind him.

'I didn't even hear that,' Agatha told her cats. 'I don't even want to have heard that.'

She carried her suitcase up to the bedroom and unpacked her clothes. She looked sadly down at all the ridiculous filmy underwear and then stuffed it all into a bag to leave in the clothes bin at Budgen's supermarket in Moreton.

After she had had a bath and changed her clothes and put on fresh make-up, she decided to visit Mrs Bloxby.

Before she left she remembered guiltily that she had sent Harry to find out about Fred's businesses in Lewisham. She phoned him up and told him to forget it.

'Why?' demanded Harry.

'Because the police say she was murdered by some associate of McNally's.'

'You believe that?'

'Yes. I'll see you in the office tomorrow.'

'Are you all right? I read about the last attempt on your life in the papers.'

'I'm fine. I'll see you tomorrow.'

The vicar seemed to delight in telling Agatha that his wife was not at home, so Agatha retreated to her cottage, heated up a portion of the casserole in the microwave and ate it at the kitchen table.

She had just finished when the doorbell rang. Again Agatha peered through the spyhole and saw Mrs Bloxby.

She flung open the door in welcome. 'My husband told me you were looking for me,' said Mrs Bloxby, 'but I was out on parish duties.' Actually, what her husband had said was, 'That bloody Raisin woman's been round here asking for you.'

'Come in. I've just eaten some of that casserole you gave me. Delicious. Thank you so much. We'll go into the sitting room. Doris has left the fire ready to be lit. What a summer! At least it's stopped people complaining about global warming.'

Agatha lit the fire. As she straightened up, that stabbing pain in her hip struck her again.

'Drink?'

'I'd like a sherry,' said Mrs Bloxby. 'I am really quite tired.'

Agatha poured her a glass and then one for herself. Mrs Bloxby sat down on the sofa and Agatha in an armchair beside the fire. 'I should use this room more,' said Agatha, looking around. 'I always seem to live in the kitchen.'

'Are you feeling all right after your adventures?'

Agatha sighed. 'I feel safe now that I'm home. It's all made me grateful for what I thought were the piffling little cases at the agency – you know, lost dogs and cats.'

'They are very important,' said Mrs Bloxby. 'Think how you would feel if your cats went missing. And how are things with James?'

'Definitely finished. Do you know he even gave me an ultimatum? He offered me this holiday trip again and said it was my last chance.'

'Oh dear.'

'It's a good thing in a way. It's brought me to my senses at last.'

'I hope you have not only finished with James but with everything to do with that dreadful place.'

'Snoth? What a name! Yes, definitely. Everything solved.'

'Including the murder of Geraldine Jankers?'

'Yes, the police have decided it was one of McNally's hit men.'

'How convenient,' murmured the vicar's wife.

'What do you mean by that?'

'It's just that it seems too neat. Perhaps it was because I was part of it for a little while.'

'For once in my life,' said Agatha, 'I'm going to accept the police decision. In fact, now that Harry and Patrick will be back at the agency,

I can relax. I might even take time off and do something with the garden.'

Mrs Bloxby sipped her drink and looked at the flames in the hearth. She knew Agatha had two obsessions. One was James Lacey and the other was danger. She wondered how long Agatha would last before she started to stir things up again.

But the weeks moved past and as the weather turned fine, Agatha showed no signs of either approaching James Lacey or worrying about Geraldine Jankers. She had told everyone in her office not to talk about the case to her. An Indian summer bathed Carsely in golden misty mornings and hot bright days.

She did pedestrian detecting during the day and sat in her garden in the warm evenings, watching her cats playing on the grass. She had hired a gardener, having decided she really did not want to do the work herself, and admired the smooth green of the lawn and the gaudy splash the dahlias made in the flowerbeds.

And then her friend Roy Silver arrived to stay one weekend. He had once worked for Agatha when she had run her own public relations firm. Agatha told him to meet her in her office on the Friday evening.

Roy appeared wearing a white Indian-style suit and leather sandals. His hair was dyed black. His face was brown with fake tan.

'What's with the Indian look?' asked Agatha.

'I'm dressing fashionably for the hot weather,' said Roy. 'Are you ready?'

'Just a few things to wrap up.' Agatha stared at her computer. 'Won't be a moment.'

'You could really do with some good magazines,' complained Roy, flicking through a pile on the coffee table in front of him. 'Dear me. Old colour supplements are not the thing.' He shifted them to one side and found a file marked 'Jankers'.

He opened it up. Harry Beam had written up everything to do with the murder of Geraldine Jankers. Roy had taken a course in speed reading and soon finished it.

'Ready,' said Agatha.

'Ready. Just been reading up on the Jankers case. Fascinating.'

'Where did you get that?'

'It was under these tatty magazines. Harry Beam's done a good job.'

'I haven't read it.'

'Why?'

'Because that case is closed.'

'Okay. Let's have dinner. I'm starving. I want to go to an Indian restaurant.'

'In that outfit? The waiters will think you're taking the piss. I feel like comfort food – roast beef, steak-and-kidney pud, that sort of thing.'

'Well, it's your waistline, duckie.'

They went to a pub called the Foxy Ferret. Roy chattered on about his latest PR ventures with a pop group called Hellish People. 'I tried to tell them the gothic look was out,' he said. 'But they insist retro-punk will soon be all the rage. Very hard to sell a line about them to the newspapers.'

'What's their music like?'

'Hellish.'

'Lost cause.'

'I hate lost causes,' said Roy petulantly. 'It's not my fault I can't publicize them, but the boss seems to think it is. Talking about lost causes – what about the Jankers case? I didn't read in the newspapers of any arrest. Who do you think did it? Cyril Hammond, who inherited close to a million? But then, how would Cyril know that Wayne would get shot so he could inherit? Fred Jankers, whose businesses were on their last legs and who got the insurance money? Or that old boy, Archie Swale, who for some reason your Harry thinks is a possible candidate?'

Agatha said in an even, measured tone, 'I won't say this again, Roy. It's over. Case solved. One of the drug baron's men did for her.'

'There was nothing about that in Harry's file.'

'Shut up about it.'

But that night, while Roy slept in the spare room, Agatha's memories of all the violence she had endured came flooding back. She remembered her fear when Brian McNally had abducted her and then when Deborah had been found shot. Once again memory dragged her back to the bar of the Palace Hotel and Brian McNally pointing a gun at her as the waves came crashing through the window.

She fell into an uneasy sleep and dreamed of being in James's arms once more, awakening at last to another sunny day and filled with longing for him.

As she went downstairs to prepare breakfast for Roy, she found all her old obsession for James was back and along with it a nagging restlessness. James, for Agatha, was as strong an addiction as cigarettes.

Roy padded into the kitchen wrapped in a gaudy Chinese dressing gown. His face was covered in black streaks.

'Your hair dye's run during the night,' said Agatha. 'Take a look. There's a mirror over the sink.'

Roy peered at his face and let out a squawk of horror. 'What am I to do?'

'Go upstairs and take a shower and shampoo all the colour out.'

While she waited for him, Agatha's mind turned over what Roy had told her about Harry's report. There had been things she had not known.

Roy appeared again half an hour later, his hair now a mousy brown and wearing a denim shirt and blue jeans.

'Really,' said Agatha, 'you look almost human.'

'I look like a nerd,' said Roy. 'What's the programme for today?'

'I might just go back to the office and look at that file.'

Chapter Twelve

Agatha had given her staff the weekend off. While Roy fidgeted around, she read the file. Harry had not bothered about Brian McNally. The whole focus of the report was on the murder of Geraldine Jankers.

When she had finished reading she looked up at Roy, who was walking about. 'I'm beginning to feel I should have asked further questions.'

Roy said, 'From all you've told me about that dreary watering hole, I've no intention of ruining my weekend by going there.'

'Nobody will be there now. The hotel will be boarded up for repairs.' Agatha went to her computer and found the list of addresses that Patrick had inveigled from his contact. Fred Jankers was in Lewisham, as was Cyril Hammond. That left only Archie Swale in Brighton.

'Let me see,' she said. 'Fred and Cyril are in Lewisham –'

'I am not, repeat *not*, going to Lewisham.'

'And Archie Swale is in Brighton.'

'Now Brighton I don't mind.'

'Maybe we could just run down there and have a word with him. It's a lovely day.'

'All right.'

In the car Roy switched on the radio to a 'golden oldies' pop station. The voice of Gloria Gaynor belting out 'I Will Survive' filled the car.

'Listen to that,' said Roy. 'She's singing your tune – the anthem of the dumped.'

'Turn it off.'

Roy switched off the radio. 'You've never mentioned James Lacey.'

'Why should I?'

'He's right next door to your cottage and yet he hasn't called, you don't speak about him, and you never looked in the direction of his cottage once.'

'That's finished. I don't want to talk about him.'

'Thank goodness for that. I feel your heart has bled enough.'

'I wonder just exactly how much Cyril got from Geraldine's will,' said Agatha. 'And how much her life was insured for. I don't think Fred killed her for the insurance. I'll bet the whole thing was her idea. She would strike a deal where she insured her life and he insured his.'

'So what has this Archie Swale got out of it? Nothing at all, if I remember Harry's report properly.'

'He's got a vile temper,' said Agatha. 'He was in the paratroopers. He's got strong wrists.'

'But how could he get her to dress and come out into the night and walk down to the beach?

Fred was in the room. There was no phone call. He says he fell asleep before she went out, but if there had been a call he would have known about it. So it must have been prearranged.'

'If it was Archie Swale,' said Agatha, 'what could he say to entice her down?'

'Maybe she liked power. Maybe she kept in touch with him. Maybe she said she was going to Snoth and he arranged to meet her, saying he had a present for her. Did you ever tell the police about those items of jewellery Geraldine had stashed under the mattress?'

'I couldn't. I would have had to tell them how I knew.'

'Harry says in his report that he's sure Fred did not know they were there.'

'Let's see what Archie has to say, although he'll probably slam the door in our faces.'

'What! You mean we're going all this way just to get a door slammed in our faces?'

'I thought you'd be delighted, Roy. Brighton is hailed as the San Francisco of the British Isles.'

'It's no use you implying I'm gay. I'm thinking of getting married. Watch out! You nearly hit that man on the pedestrian crossing.'

'You amaze me. Who's the lucky girl?'

'I haven't got one yet.'

'So why get married?'

'It's my boss, Mr Pedman. He only invites members of staff to parties at his home if they're married.'

'You can't just get married to please your boss and go to a few parties.'

'I want to further my career,' said Roy primly. 'There are plenty of single girls out there.'

'Think hard about it before you do anything,' said Agatha. 'I mean, you could find a nice quiet girl and then, after you were married, she might start to bully the life out of you. What about children? I can't see you with children.'

'Then you know bugger all about me. Drive.'

To Agatha's amazement, not only was Archie Swale at home, but he actually seemed pleased to see them.

'Come in,' he said. 'It's Mrs Raisin, isn't it?'

'Yes, and this is my young friend, Roy Silver,' said Agatha, heartily glad that Roy was not wearing his Indian outfit.

'I was just about to have a little tincture,' he said. 'Drink?'

'I'm driving,' said Agatha. 'Oh, well, one won't hurt. I'll have a gin and tonic.'

He went over to a small side table laden with bottles. 'I've no tonic, but I do have bitters. What about a pink gin?'

'No, thank you. Sherry will do if you have any.'

'Yes, I do. What about you, young man?'

'The same.'

When the drinks were served and they were all seated, Archie said, 'I'm so glad that dreadful case is solved. Poor Geraldine. I didn't like the woman, but I would have gone on wondering who killed her. I remember when I was in Northern Ireland . . .' His voice droned on in a long

237

military anecdote while Agatha wondered how she could ask him some pertinent questions.

A fly buzzed against the window. The room was hot and stuffy. Agatha was beginning to feel as trapped as the fly.

Then she realized he was asking, 'Would you like to see my medals?'

'Very much,' said Agatha.

Archie staggered slightly as he rose to his feet and Agatha thought, he's been drinking a lot before we arrived.

'Now, where did I put them?' Roy stifled a yawn as Archie jerked open drawers on his desk. Agatha stared numbly at a picture over the fireplace. Then, as Archie jerked open another drawer, Agatha saw reflected in the glass of the picture a flash of brilliance. Archie slammed a door of the desk shut violently, muttering, 'Not that drawer.'

'Maybe you keep them in the bedside table,' said Agatha. 'I often keep mementos there.'

'I'll go and look. It's my memory these days. I can remember things from a long time ago but I can hardly remember what happened yesterday.'

When he had left the room, Agatha moved quickly and quietly to that desk. He had been bending over. Must be one of the bottom drawers. She opened the one on the left. Nothing but papers. She opened the one on the right and stifled a gasp as she looked down at a blaze of jewels – necklaces, bracelets and watches, all glittering like the treasure trove in an illustration to a child's detective story. She heard Archie's slow

238

step on the stairs, shut the drawer quietly and regained her seat just in time.

'I can't figure it out,' said Archie, coming into the room. 'Blessed if I can remember where I put them. What about another drink?'

'Nothing for us,' said Agatha. 'We really must be going. I only called to see if you were all right.'

She and Roy stood up. 'Can't I persuade you to stay?' he pleaded, loneliness shining in his old eyes.

'No, honestly. Thanks for the drink. Come along, Roy.'

Outside, Agatha said urgently, 'I've got to phone Barret at Snoth.'

'Who's he?'

'The detective inspector who was in charge of the case.'

'Why?'

Agatha turned and then waved. 'He's watching us from the window. Wait until we get into the car.'

'You've got a ticket,' said Roy, removing it from under the wiper. 'This is a residents' parking area.'

'I'll pay it gladly. Get in.'

Once they were in the car, Agatha drove off. 'I want to phone when we're out of sight. Roy, in that bottom drawer were piles of jewels. Don't you see? Geraldine probably gave them to him for safekeeping, keeping back a few bits and pieces for herself under the mattress. So there's a prearrangement to meet her on the beach and

239

hand over the jewels. But he strangles her instead. Let's stop in the car park of this pub and I'll phone Barret.'

James Lacey had seen Agatha drive off with Roy. He wondered what she was up to. He still could not quite believe that the formerly adoring Agatha was avoiding him so completely. He had been reluctant to go off on holiday on his own and so had returned to Carsely. Immediately after his return, every time his doorbell rang he answered it, sure he would find Agatha on his doorstep. But it was always either the postman with a parcel or one of the village women with a cake for him.

He went along to the village stores and saw Mrs Bloxby just leaving. He hailed her.

'What's Agatha up to these days?' he asked.

'My dear Mr Lacey, why don't you ask her yourself? She lives right next door to you.'

James burst out, 'She's not talking to me!'

'Then perhaps you should talk to her,' said Mrs Bloxby mildly. 'Now, if you will excuse me . . .'

And I hope you never do climb down off your high horse and speak to her, thought Mrs Bloxby. Mrs Raisin has suffered enough.

Agatha had made her phone call. How long would it take Barret to get a search warrant, and on a Saturday, too?

Roy and Agatha casually walked back to the square and watched Archie's house from a safe distance.

The sky was darkening and they had not eaten anything. Roy was starting to complain loudly.

Agatha capitulated. They went back to the pub for beer and sandwiches, but then Agatha insisted they return to the square one more time.

This time, there were a police car and an unmarked car outside Archie's house. They watched and waited.

Suddenly the door opened and Archie was led out and put into the police car. Barret and Wilkins followed, got into the unmarked car and drove off.

'Good, now back to Carsely,' said Roy.

'No,' said Agatha. 'We're going to Snoth.'

'Correction, sweetie. *You're* going to Snoth. I'm going back to Carsely to get my stuff. Drop me at the station.'

'Roy, you may as well come with me. It'll take you ages to get to Carsely. Train to Victoria, tube to Paddington, train to Moreton-in-Marsh and then taxi to Carsely.'

'Oh, all right,' said Roy sulkily. 'But don't be all night over it.'

A police car stopped them on the road out of Brighton. 'You are to follow us to Snoth police station,' she was instructed.

'I was going there anyway,' said Agatha cheerfully.

* * *

241

At the police station Agatha was told to wait. They wanted a statement from her.

So she and Roy waited and waited while the muffled sound of the rising tide reached their ears.

'What's happening about the sea wall?' Agatha asked the desk sergeant.

'They're building a new high one, and about time, too. The hotel's finished. Pity, that. I remember it as a boy. Grand place, it was.'

'Mrs Raisin?' A policewoman appeared. 'Will you and your companion follow me?'

Agatha and Roy were buzzed through and followed the policewoman to an interview room.

Barret and Wilkins were there. A feeling of familiar fatigue assailed Agatha as the tape was switched on and the questioning began.

At one point Barret asked, 'How could you possibly believe that there were the jewels in that drawer because of a single flash of light you saw reflected in the glass of a painting?'

'The sun was shining brightly into the room,' said Agatha, 'and that reflected glitter got me thinking it might be the missing jewels.' She waved one arm expansively. 'The way I see it is that Swale was given the jewels by Geraldine for safekeeping. But he doesn't want to give them back. So he lures her on to the beach. Probably arranged it beforehand. That is one good solid reason why she would leave her hotel room in the middle of the night.'

Said Barret, 'Mr Swale insists that Mrs Jankers did give him the jewels to look after. He did not know anything about the theft. He meant to deliver them to her solicitor, but forgot about them.'

'You can't forget about a drawerful of gems!'

'Nonetheless, he is sticking to his story. We will probably charge him with harbouring stolen property, although even that's doubtful because he's sticking to his story that he did not know the stuff had been stolen, but apart from that we have no evidence whatsoever that he committed the murder. You should really leave detecting to the police.'

'Oh really? Would you have found the jewels?'

'Sooner or later,' said Barret.

'That's a load of rubbish. Are the jewels from that robbery?'

'Swale tried to say at first that they were from an aunt of his, but we had the record of the stolen stuff faxed over and, yes, they're from the robbery. When we asked him why he had invented the aunt, he said Geraldine had sworn him to secrecy and he was honouring her memory.'

'And you believe that?' raged Agatha.

'Interview ended,' said Barret, switching off the tape. 'You are free to go, Mrs Raisin. Just stay out of it.'

'And that's all the thanks I get!' complained Agatha on the road home.

Roy stifled a yawn. 'So you keep saying over and over again. Let it go.'

Agatha drove on for several miles. Then she said, 'Of course I could be wrong. Swale might not be the murderer. I would like to go and see Cyril Hammond.'

'If you want me to go with you to Lewisham tomorrow, the answer's still no.'

'I tell you what,' said Agatha, 'I'll run you up to London tomorrow and then I'll go to Lewisham.'

'On your own?'

'No, I'll see if Harry will come with me.'

Harry was delighted at the prospect when she phoned him the next morning. Agatha was relieved. She had been sure that a young man like Harry would have a busy social life. She did not know Harry had cheerfully cancelled a date with his latest girlfriend and was glad of an excuse to do so, as his interest in her had been wearing thin.

They dropped Roy at his home in Fulham and then made their way to Lewisham.

'Where does Cyril live?' asked Agatha.

'Perry Way. I'll direct you. Haven't been there, but I looked up directions before in case we needed them.'

Cyril's home was in a row of terraced houses. Two children were playing in the weedy front garden.

'Must have visitors,' said Agatha, ringing the bell.

A tired-looking woman with a baby on her hip answered the door.

'Mr Hammond?' asked Agatha.

'Don't live here any more. We bought the house from him.'

'Do you know where he lives now?'

'Wait there. Got the address somewhere. Here, hold the baby.'

Agatha clutched hold of the baby, which began to cry. 'Let me,' said Harry, taking the baby from her and starting to talk nonsense to it. The baby gurgled happily and sucked its thumb.

After a while the woman came back and handed them a piece of paper which had grease spots on it.

They thanked her, Harry handed back the baby, and they left.

'So where is he?' asked Harry.

'He's moved to Swindon. I hate Swindon. I always get lost in the roundabouts.'

'Should we go there, or try to see Fred Jankers now we're here?'

'Maybe. But I'd really like to see Cyril. My money's on him.'

'I'll drive if we go to Swindon.'

Agatha capitulated, and Harry drove off.

'It'll be interesting to know what state of mind Cyril's in,' said Harry. 'It's a hell of a way to Swindon. It'll take us nearly three hours.'

On they went through Forest Hill, Dulwich, Streatham, Clapham, Wandsworth Common, East Putney, Kew Bridge, the traffic hell of the Chiswick Roundabout, and then, with a sigh of relief, Harry drove down on to the M4.

'I'd better drive into the centre of Swindon

and ask for directions,' said Harry. 'What's that address again?'

Agatha fished the greasy piece of paper out of her handbag. 'Tullis House, Maycombe Avenue.'

Harry lowered the window and asked various passers-by, but no one seemed to recognize the address.

He drove on a bit, seemingly happily oblivious to the angry hooting of horns from cars behind him every time he stopped. Then he cried, 'Oh, look, there's a copper on the beat. Haven't seen one of those in years.' He stopped and asked the policeman for directions.

Agatha was glad she wasn't driving. She could never have remembered all these turn-rights and turn-lefts.

She sat silently while Harry weaved his way competently through street after street out to the outskirts of Swindon.

'Here we are,' he said at last. 'Gosh, they must have got their hands on Geraldine's money pretty fast.'

They had expected Tullis House would turn out to be a block of flats, but it was a large white villa in a street of equally large white villas. Harry drove up the short driveway at the front and then parked. 'If he's not at home,' said Harry, 'I'll scream.'

Agatha felt that awful pain in her hip and swung her right leg out of the car by putting one hand under her hip to support it.

Harry rang the doorbell and they waited. The Indian summer day bathed everything in a golden glow. Then they could hear light footsteps approaching the door. A pretty young Asian woman stood smiling at them. She had skin as golden as the day and she had long black hair down to her waist.

'Mr Hammond?' asked Agatha.

'You are friends of his?'

'Just tell him Mrs Raisin is here to see him.'

The girl giggled and covered her mouth with her hand. 'Such a funny name.'

'What's so funny about it?' asked Agatha as the girl pattered off into the house.

'I suppose it's a bit like being called Mrs Prune.'

'No, it is not!' said Agatha huffily. 'And who is this, anyway? Has he got himself a maid?'

The girl came back. 'Please to come in.'

She shut the door behind them and led the way to a sitting room on the ground floor. Cyril was waiting to meet them.

'Nice to see you again,' he said. 'You've met Lin.'

The sitting room was furnished with Victorian chairs and a Victorian sofa. Dull landscapes in need of cleaning hung on the walls. A portrait of a severe-looking woman in a black gown and lace cap hung over the marble fireplace. Agatha guessed that Cyril had bought the contents along with the house.

'Sit down,' said Cyril. 'Like a drink?'

'Just coffee,' said Agatha. Harry said he would have the same. Cyril nodded to Lin, who hurried off.

'Where's Dawn?' asked Agatha.

'We broke up. We're getting a divorce. I'll be marrying Lin as soon as the divorce comes through.'

'Where did you meet Lin?'

'Chinese restaurant in Swindon. Love at first sight. What brings you?'

'I don't know if it's in the papers yet,' said Agatha, easing herself down on to the sofa and trying not to wince. 'Archie Swale was arrested yesterday.'

'Geraldine's ex! Why?'

'He had a drawerful of jewellery. Turns out to be the jewellery from that theft.'

Lin came in with a laden tray. The cups rattled as Cyril shouted, 'The old bitch! She told me Charlie had hidden the jewels after giving a few pieces to Wayne. She said she didn't know where they were.' He suddenly calmed down, and taking out a gaudy silk handkerchief, mopped his brow.

Lin cast him nervous little looks as she poured cups of coffee.

'Go away and do something,' Cyril ordered her. Lin scurried from the room, her head bent.

'I thought I knew everything there was to know about Geraldine,' said Cyril, sinking down into an armchair. 'We were childhood sweethearts.'

'Why didn't you marry her?' asked Harry.

'Because at that time we had no money and Geraldine wanted money and what Geraldine wanted, Geraldine got. But Archie Swale! She despised him. She thought she'd married into money and then found out he had pretty much only his pension.'

'I can't understand it either,' said Agatha. 'I could swear Archie hated her. Why would she let him have the jewellery?'

'Perhaps because she hit another bum one with Fred Jankers. I remember her telling me he had this chain of dress shops. But the shops weren't doing much business. She tried to get him to sell the lot, but he stuck his heels in and said his father had started the business and he was damned if he would sell even one shop. Wait a bit. Archie must have murdered her. That's why she went out in the middle of the night. Of course she'd go, knowing he had the jewellery.'

'Trouble is,' said Harry, 'the police don't have a shred of evidence.'

'Why wouldn't Geraldine sell the jewels if she liked money that much?' asked Agatha.

'The stuff was hot. She would guess if she held on to it for a long time, she could then get rid of it bit by bit. But Archie! I can't get over it. I was her friend. She'd still be alive if she'd asked me to keep them.'

'You mean you would have kept stolen goods?' asked Agatha.

'What else could I have done? I wouldn't have turned her over to the police.'

Said Agatha, 'I gather she left you comfortably off. How did she manage to amass so much money?'

'May as well tell you, now she's dead. When she was only a teenager, she was gorgeous-looking. She went on the game. Got picked up by a rich businessman who kept her in a flat in Chelsea. When he got tired of her she threatened to tell his wife and so he paid her off. He'd put the flat in her name and she sold it. Then she decided she wanted marriage and kids. By that time I was married to Dawn, so she married Jimmy, who had a good bit of cash and left it all to her when he died. She went back on the game and got herself another rich man. He was the kind who thinks criminals are glamorous. He took her to Marbella and she met Charlie Black there. Fell hook, line and sinker, she did, especially when he promised to bring up Jimmy's boy, Wayne, as if he were his own. But she'd got to know a stockbroker and had invested her money and she was too canny to let Charlie get his hands on it. She went off him after a bit and kept complaining she'd left a rich man for him. So he planned the jewel theft. Silly bugger got caught.'

'Where's Dawn living?' asked Harry.

'Why?'

'Just thought we might want to tell her the news as well.'

'Here.' Cyril took out a notebook and scribbled down an address. 'Thanks for giving me the news, but if there isn't anything else . . .'

'No, we'll go now,' said Agatha, wishing she had not sunk so far down into the feathery cushions of the sofa. But when she rose, there was no pain. All I need is more exercise, she thought. I'm damned if I'm getting a hip replacement. No ageing.

Outside in the car she said to Harry, 'Let's look at this address. If it's in Lewisham, I'll give up for the day.'

She read the note. 'No, it's here in Swindon.'

'I saw a newsagent's a few streets away,' said Harry. 'I'll nip in and buy an *A to Z* street directory. What's the address?'

'Flat five, Wemley Court, Burford Street.'

At the newsagent's Harry bought a street directory and studied it. 'Other side of town, but we may as well go while we're here. I'm starving.'

'Let's see Dawn first and then we'll eat.'

Wemley Court turned out to be a block of council flats. Flat five was mercifully only one floor up because the lift was broken, its inner walls covered in graffiti.

Dawn opened the door to them. She seemed to have aged and her face was bare of make-up. 'Oh, it's you,' she said. 'What do you want?'

'May we come in?'

'If you must.'

The flat smelt of stale food and unwashed clothes.

'How did you end up like this?' asked Agatha. 'Isn't Cyril obliged to give you some money?'

'He beat the hell out of me,' said Dawn, 'and said unless I settled for nothing, he'd kill me.'

251

'My dear girl, get yourself to the Citizens Advice Bureau, get legal aid and sue the pants off him.'

'I can't.'

'Why?' demanded Agatha.

'I'm afraid of him. Leave me alone. Why did you come?'

Agatha told her about Archie Swale.

'Good for him,' said Dawn, lighting a cheap cigarette. 'I've often wanted to kill her myself.'

'Would Cyril have killed her?'

'Him? He thought the sun shone out of her fat arse.'

'Look, here, Dawn, when he beat you up you should have gone straight to the police.'

She hugged her thin body with her skinny arms. 'I just want to forget about the whole thing.'

'One more thing. If Cyril had asked Geraldine to meet him on the beach in the middle of the night, would she have gone?'

'Sure, she would.'

'Did he leave the room that night?'

'I told the police he didn't, but the fact is I'd had a lot to drink and then I took sleeping pills.'

They could not get any more information out of her and left.

'Food!' said Harry. 'And lots of it.'

After a substantial meal they decided to leave calling on Fred until the following day.

Back in Carsely, Agatha fussed over her cats

and then returned to studying Harry's file. Cyril was the prime candidate. He must have known Geraldine meant to leave her money to him. Now he had ruthlessly got rid of poor Dawn and had found a pretty little Chinese girlfriend.

Agatha planned to return to Dawn in the near future and see if she could do anything for her. Maybe she would get her a good lawyer.

She could almost sense the presence of James Lacey next door, distracting her from concentrating on the file. For the first time, she hoped he would keep away from her. Her intelligence told her it would be madness to go down that obsessive road again. Her emotions nagged at her, mourning the loss of that very obsession.

What could she say to Fred Jankers to prompt some sort of lead? Perhaps the best idea would be to ask him questions about Cyril and to take him back over the night of Geraldine's murder. Maybe he remembered something now that he had not told the police.

The doorbell rang, making her jump nervously. She went quietly to the front door and peered through the spyhole. She saw the face of James, distorted by the glass of the spyhole.

She reached out for the doorknob and then drew her hand back.

Agatha retreated to her desk. The doorbell went again. She nervously lit a cigarette.

Then she faintly heard his footsteps retreating and her shoulders relaxed.

The phone rang. She stiffened up again, waiting until the ringing stopped. After a few minutes she went and picked up the receiver. She was told there was a message for her, press one. She pressed one. 'You have one message,' said the voice of British Telecom. 'Message received at ten twenty-five p.m.' James's voice started to speak. 'Agatha, I know you are home. Why . . .' Agatha held the phone away from her ear so that she could just hear when he had finished speaking without hearing the rest of the words. When he had finished, she pressed button three on the receiver to cancel the message in case she might be tempted to listen to it later.

Agatha silently cursed James as she and Harry drove off the next morning. He was invading her thoughts, and already part of her brain was wishing she hadn't cancelled that message.

'Penny for them,' said Harry.

'I was just wondering what to ask Fred,' Agatha lied.

'Maybe ask him about Cyril,' suggested Harry. 'That might get him to open up a bit.'

'Good idea,' said Agatha, just as if she hadn't thought of it already. 'Mind you, it might have been a better idea to phone him first. It's a long way to Lewisham and now the working week has started, the traffic will be hellish. What if he's not at home?'

'Then we'll just need to hang around until he comes back,' said Harry cheerfully.

*   *   *

Fred Jankers was not only at home but seemed glad to see them. 'Come in,' he hailed them. 'I get a bit lonely these days.'

His house appeared much cleaner than when Harry had last seen it. Fred fussed around, making them tea and producing a plate of biscuits. When they were all settled, Agatha began.

'We went to see Cyril Hammond yesterday.'

Fred's face darkened. 'That shyster! Getting all Geraldine's money.'

'Just as well you got the insurance,' said Agatha.

'Geraldine told me she was leaving everything to me. She even showed me the will.'

'Have you got that will?'

'No, she took it away again. Said she was leaving it with the solicitor.'

'Maybe the will leaving everything to Wayne and then to Cyril if Wayne died was an old one?'

'Can't be. She drew up that will leaving everything to me right before we went on our honeymoon.'

Asked Agatha, 'Did you never think that Cyril might have murdered her?'

'No. The police say it must have been one of Brian McNally's men.'

Harry said, 'We were just wondering, now that it's all over, if you happened to remember something about that night that might have escaped your memory up until now?'

'Can't remember a thing except falling asleep and then waking up to the news that she was dead. I'm a heavy sleeper.'

255

Fred looked at them, a glint of suspicion in his eyes. 'Why are you two still ferreting around? The case is closed. Geraldine's murder was the result of clever planning. A pair of amateurs like you will never find out if anyone did it apart from that drug baron.'

'If you thought we were so amateurish,' said Agatha, 'why did you ask me to investigate?'

'I was in shock and grasping at straws.'

'How did you feel when you read in the papers that Archie Swale had been arrested?'

He goggled at her. 'What! I haven't been reading the newspapers.'

'He had a drawerful of jewellery from that robbery that Charlie Black committed. Thousands of pounds' worth of stuff. Geraldine had given it to him for safekeeping.'

Fred jumped to his feet and began to pace up and down the room. 'That bitch,' he said savagely. 'She told me she was loaded. Why else do you think I married a tart like that? Told me she would see me all right. Then that ghastly so-called honeymoon and I learn I'm to pay for bloody Wayne, creepy Cyril and their wives. Now all I hear is that she was out to see everyone all right except me.'

Agatha felt suddenly calm. All the bits of the jigsaw seemed to be clicking into place.

'You murdered her,' said Agatha. 'How did you get her down to the beach? Did you suggest a romantic walk in the moonlight because you had a present for her, say, a valuable present?'

He sat down again, his head drooping, staring at the floor. 'You'll never prove it.'

Heart beating hard, Agatha said gently, 'I know. But you'll feel better for telling someone. You're quite right. There's no proof. You must have been awfully clever.'

He raised his head. 'I was, wasn't I? I found those bits of jewellery under the mattress and I knew immediately where they must have come from because she actually seemed proud of having been married to a villain. So I told her I knew something that would put her in prison, but I didn't want to tell her in the hotel. I suggested a walk.

'When we were down on the beach, I told her I had found those items of jewellery under the mattress and if she didn't pay me off handsomely and give me a divorce, I would go straight to the police and turn her in for harbouring stolen property.

'She started to howl insults at me, sexual insults, coarse and horrible. She turned her back on me and said over her shoulder, "I'll tell Cyril and Wayne. You little wimp, by the time they're finished with you, you won't dare go near any police station."

'That bright scarf was fluttering behind her in the breeze. I seized the ends and twisted them and twisted them, hearing her gurgle. I was mad with rage. I only meant to frighten her or something. I don't know now. I only know I wanted to shut that awful jeering voice up. She fell silent. I dropped her down on to the beach.

'I ran back to the hotel. That night receptionist was nowhere in sight. I ran all the way to our room, took strong sleeping pills and went to bed. So now you've got what you want, you can leave. Oh, you can tell the police, but I'll deny every word and they've no proof. Get out!'

Agatha jumped to her feet and backed away. Fred was no longer a pathetic little figure, but a madman capable of anything.

She and Harry ran to their car and got in. Agatha drove off and stopped round the corner.

'Who would have thought it? We've no proof, he's right about that, but I'm going to tell the police anyway.'

Harry grinned. 'Oh, we've got proof of every word. I'm wired for sound.' He opened his jacket. There was a tape recorder against his chest which he had hung round his neck with two strings.

'Oh, Harry Beam, I love you!' cried Agatha, giving him a hearty kiss on the mouth.

'That's all right,' mumbled Harry, turning away but not quickly enough to hide the fact from Agatha that he was wiping his mouth.

Epilogue

Agatha scanned the newspapers during the next few days looking for any reports of an arrest.

She was just on the point of phoning Barret when Bill Wong arrived. 'I've got news for you,' he said, settling himself in a kitchen chair with her cats.

'About time,' said Agatha. 'I was just about to phone Barret. Has Jankers been arrested?'

He shook his head. 'After you delivered that tape, they sent Lewisham police to bring him in. There was no reply but his car was parked outside. They broke down the door and found him as dead as a doornail. He had taken an overdose.'

'Did he leave a letter, a confession?'

'Nothing.'

'Okay, so he's dead. So why was there nothing about him being the murderer in the newspapers?'

'The case was considered already closed and the police want to keep it that way. So no statement to the newspapers. Barret doesn't want to look a fool and have to explain how a Gloucestershire detective agency managed to find out what he could not. Anyway, praise from me, Agatha. Good work. There's something else. Ages ago, a girl accused Jankers of rape, but he managed to get off with it.'

'So Mrs Bloxby was right,' said Agatha. 'She said that subconsciously Geraldine would be attracted to villains.

'I suppose I'm glad it's all over. But I must give praise where it's due. If Harry Beam hadn't continued to research the case, I'd never have got back on to it.'

Bill looked amused. 'Where's the old Agatha gone who would have taken all the praise herself?'

'I'm not like that,' said Agatha huffily, 'and never was.'

'Talking about a changed Agatha, how's James?'

'He's in his small corner and I'm in mine.'

'He isn't in his corner any more. He's gone.'

'How do you know?'

'You weren't in earlier, so I knocked at his door for a chat. No reply and no car. So I went to the village stores to get a soft drink and they told me he'd dropped in to buy the papers and said he was going abroad.'

Now Agatha desperately wished she hadn't cancelled that message.

James drove steadily to Heathrow Airport to catch a flight to Istanbul on his way to the holiday resorts of southern Turkey. He had been commissioned to write another travel book. If Agatha hadn't been so stupid, she could have come with him. Why wouldn't she answer her phone when he called?

He had planned to stay overnight in Istanbul. He decided he would write to her from there.

Cyril Hammond turned up the volume on the television set to drown out the sobs of Lin, whom he had locked in the bedroom after having given her a sound thrashing with a leather belt. The feeling of power and euphoria that the administered beating had given him was fast evaporating. To his relief, the sobbing suddenly stopped.

In the bedroom, Lin dried her eyes. Cyril would never let her use the phone, but her brother had given her a tiny mobile phone for emergencies just before she had moved in with Cyril. As soon as she was settled in, Cyril had told her she was not to go out without his permission or make any phone calls, and then the beatings had started. She had endured them for too long, hoping always that he would change. Lin fished under the mattress where she had hidden the phone and called her brother at his Chinese restaurant and began to whisper rapidly in Mandarin.

Half an hour later, Cyril decided it was time to let Lin out. He would caress her and apologize as he had done so many times before.

He had just risen to his feet when he heard the

doorbell ring. The door had thick stained-glass panels and all he could see was a shadowy figure through them.

He opened the door on the chain. He recognized Lin's brother, Chang.

'I've come to see my sister,' said Chang politely.

'What a pity. She's gone out.'

'Let me in.'

'It's not convenient.'

'Very well. I will return another time.'

Cyril closed the door with a sigh of relief.

He was just walking away when he heard a loud crack. He swung round in alarm. Chang stood there, the crow bar he had used to lever the door open in one hand. Crowding behind him came six Chinese men.

'Lin!' called Chang.

She screamed something in Mandarin. While his Chinese followers held Cyril, Chang ran up to the bedroom and cracked the door open.

Lin flung herself into his arms. Then she stood back and solemnly lifted her T-shirt, showing black, blue and yellow bruises.

Chang ordered her to wait in the bedroom and went downstairs. On his orders, the men dragged Cyril, crying and howling, into the sitting room.

'You,' said Chang in English, 'are going to get a taste of what you did to my sister.'

Three weekends later, Agatha decided to brave the roundabouts of Swindon on her own and offer Dawn the services of a lawyer. After about five wrong turns, she eventually found the block of flats.

But there was no reply when she knocked at the door. A neighbour came out.

'You looking for Dawn?' she asked.

'Yes.'

'She's gone back to her husband.'

'What!'

'You heard me.'

Agatha still had Harry's *A to Z* in the car. She managed to find her way back to Tullis House, went up and rang the bell.

The door was opened by Dawn, a Dawn in expensive clothes and with her face heavily made up.

'How could you go back?' asked Agatha. 'I came down to offer you the services of a lawyer. He'll just hurt you again.'

'He won't be hurting anyone. He's just out of the hospital. Come in and see for yourself.'

Wondering, Agatha followed her into the sitting room. Cyril was sitting in a wheelchair by the window, his head bandaged and both legs and arms in plaster.

'What happened?' asked Agatha as Cyril stared at her dully.

'Come through to the kitchen and I'll tell you.'

In the kitchen, Dawn poured herself a stiff measure of Southern Comfort. 'Not for me,' said Agatha, waving away the offered bottle. 'I'm driving.'

So Dawn told her between sips of Southern

Comfort what had happened to Cyril. 'I've got a nurse to look after him,' she said, 'and a personal therapist comes every day.'

'Didn't he report them to the police?'

'The brother, Chang, said if he did they would kill him next time.'

'So how did you get back with him?'

'He phoned me from the hospital. He said he should never have left me.'

'Dawn, when he's all mended up, he might start beating you again.'

She grinned. 'I made friends with Lin and she told me to phone her if he ever laid a finger on me again. Oh, it's great to have all this money.'

Agatha returned home to find Charles waiting for her. 'When did you get here?' she asked.

'Early this morning.' Charles still had a set of keys to Agatha's cottage. 'I picked up your mail and put it on the kitchen table. Then I cruised around and had some lunch in Moreton.'

'So what brings you?'

'Just felt restless. Also, I was wondering about the murder of Geraldine Jankers.'

'Her husband did it.'

'Nothing in the papers.'

'The police are keeping quiet about it. He committed suicide.'

'So were you the one that found out?'

Agatha told him about that confession and how Harry had taped it.

'But how did you suddenly decide to accuse him of the murder?'

Agatha said, 'I could have been wrong. But it was when he admitted that he thought Geraldine had money, and he seemed so viciously furious with her, that it all seemed to click into place. It was bright of Harry. Once I got a confession out of Fred and he said I could never prove it, that's when Harry told me he had taped the whole thing. I don't know what I'm going to do without him. The university term will be starting soon.'

'Where's he going?'

'Cambridge. I had hoped he would go to Oxford and then at least I could have dropped in to see him.'

'He can always work for you in the holidays. How's James?'

'Gone off abroad.'

'Without a fond goodbye?'

'He tried. But I don't want to go back through all that misery again.'

Charles stretched and yawned. 'Don't know why I'm so tired. I'm off to Cheltenham to do some shopping. Like to come?'

'I'd better get into the office.'

'Then I'll see you this evening. We'll go out for dinner. Pick you up at eight.'

When he had left, Agatha went through to the kitchen and flipped through the post which had arrived that morning. She found herself staring down at a letter with a Turkish stamp.

She ripped it open. It was from James.

'Dear Agatha,' she read. 'I am sorry I could not get a chance to speak to you before I left. I wanted to ask you to come with me. I thought we might have fun touring the southern Turkish holiday resorts together. But I am enclosing my itinerary and the dates when I will be in each place in the hope that you might like to fly out and join me. Love, James.'

Agatha sat down slowly. She read the letter over and over again. She looked at the attached itinerary. The longing to get the next plane out was fierce. This must be what a drug addict feels, she thought sadly, when she's craving her next fix.

Then she carried the letter through to the sitting room and put it in the fireplace and struck a match. She sat back on her heels and watched the letter burn.

One tear rolled down her cheek.

She felt she was attending the cremation of a dearly loved friend.

James Lacey sat on the balcony of his hotel in Izmir. He could see the hotel entrance below. Taxis came and went. People got out with luggage. He found himself hoping against hope that a familiar stocky figure would get out of one of those cabs.

He was due to move on the next day. Would she come? But he felt he no longer knew Agatha.

He had always been self-sufficient, enjoying his own company. But for the first time in his life, as another taxi drew up and a family got out, he felt lonely.

Agatha settled into the daily grind of work at the detective agency. There were no dramatic cases; most were from people hoping for a divorce and looking for proof of adultery. But the agency was paying its way at last.

Charles dropped in and out of her life as he had always done. The evenings were dark early and the branches of the trees were becoming bare.

She visited Mrs Bloxby one Saturday evening.

'If you will forgive me for saying so,' said Mrs Bloxby, 'you are not looking your usual self.'

'I've been working hard on a lot of dreary cases, that's all.'

'Perhaps you should take a holiday.'

'Where?'

'Somewhere sunny. The heat would ease that pain in your hip.'

'What pain?'

'Mrs Raisin, arthritis is not just going to go away. Don't leave a hip replacement to the last minute.'

'It's not that bad,' said Agatha. 'I'll think about it.'

When Agatha had left, Mrs Bloxby stood at the doorway of the village and watched her walking off slowly down the cobbled street.

'Poor Mrs Raisin,' murmured the vicar's wife. 'She's missing James quite dreadfully.'

Agatha turned into Lilac Lane and then stopped short. The lights were on in James's cottage and smoke was rising above the thatch from the chimney. She walked forward, paused, and then walked forward again.

This is stupid, she thought.

But she went up to his door, her heart beating hard, and rang the bell.

Read about Agatha's first attempts at sleuthing in . . .

Agatha Raisin and the Quiche of Death

High-flying public relations supremo Agatha Raisin has decided to take early retirement. She's off to make a new life in a picture-perfect Cotswold village. To make new friends, she enters the local quiche-making competition – and to secure the first prize she secretly pays a visit to a London deli. When the judge succumbs after tasting her quiche, Agatha is revealed as a cheat and a potential murderer. She must turn amateur sleuth in order to clear her name and avoid a prison cell.

£5.99 paperback

Agatha Raisin and the Vicious Vet

Attractive new vet, Paul Bladen, has taken a shine to Agatha but before romance can blossom, Paul is killed in an accident with Lord Pendlebury's horse. However, the circumstances are suspicious so Agatha decides to play sleuth once more with the help of her stand-offish neighbour, James Lacey. As usual Agatha rushes in, heedless of the lurking menace to both of them . . .

£5.99 paperback

Praise for M. C. Beaton and the Agatha Raisin series

'M. C. Beaton's imperfect heroine is an absolute gem'
Publishers Weekly

'Warning: Once you read one of Beaton's books, you're hooked' *Romantic Times*

For more information on the series go to
www.agatharaisin.co.uk

A Load of Old Bones

by Suzette Hill

Dire doings at the vicarage!

A Load of Old Bones takes a nostalgic romp through 1950s mythical Surrey, where murky deeds and shady characters abound! All that Reverend Francis Oughterard had ever wanted was an easy life and a bit of peace and quiet. Instead, he gets entangled in a nightmare world of accidental murder, predatory female parishioners, officious policemen, oddball clerics, wrathful old ladies and a drunken bishop. As the vicar's life spirals out of control it is up to his supercilious cat and bone-obsessed hound to help save his skin . . .

Praise for *A Load of Old Bones*

'I think this is tremendous – amusing and professional'   Dame Beryl Bainbridge

'An enchanting tale, beautifully written, full of fun, wit and insight'
                    The very Reverend Alex Witherspoon,
                    Dean Emeritus of Guildford

Publication June 2007
£18.99

No. of copies	Order	Title	RRP	Total
		Agatha Raisin and the Quiche of Death	£5.99	
		Agatha Raisin and the Vicious Vet	£5.99	
		Agatha Raisin and the Potted Gardener	£5.99	
		Agatha Raisin and the Walkers of Dembley	£5.99	
		Agatha Raisin and the Murderous Marriage	£5.99	
		Agatha Raisin and the Terrible Tourist	£5.99	
		Agatha Raisin and the Wellspring of Death	£5.99	
		Agatha Raisin and the Wizard of Evesham	£5.99	
		Agatha Raisin and the Witch of Wyckhadden	£5.99	
		Agatha Raisin and the Fairies of Fryfam	£5.99	
		Agatha Raisin and the Love from Hell	£5.99	
		Agatha Raisin and the Day the Floods Came	£5.99	
		Agatha Raisin and the Curious Curate	£5.99	
		Agatha Raisin and the Haunted House	£5.99	
		Agatha Raisin and the Deadly Dance	£5.99	
		Agatha Raisin and the Perfect Paragon	£5.99	
		Grand Total		£

Please feel free to order any other titles that do not appear on this order form!

Name: _____

Address: _____

_____ Postcode: _____

Daytime Tel. No./Email: _____
(in case of query)

Three ways to pay:

1. *For express service telephone the TBS order line on 01206 255 800 and quote 'AR'. Order lines are open Monday–Friday, 8:30am–5:30pm*

2. I enclose a cheque made payable to **TBS Ltd** for £ _____

3. Please charge my ☐ Visa ☐ Mastercard ☐ Amex ☐ Switch

    (Switch issue no. _____)

    Card number: _____

    Expiry date: _____ Signature: _____
    (your signature is essential when paying by credit card)

Please return forms (*no stamp required*) to, FREEPOST RLUL-SJGC-SGKJ, Cash Sales/Direct Mail Dept, The Book Service, Colchester Road, Frating, Colchester CO7 7DW.

Enquiries to: readers@constablerobinson.com
www.constablerobinson.com

Constable and Robinson Ltd (directly or via its agents) may mail, email or phone you about promotions or products.
☐ Tick box if you do not want these from us ☐ or our subsidiaries